LIVE LIKE YOU WERE DYING

LIVE LIKE YOU WERE DYING

a story about living

Michael Morris

WestBow
P R E S S

A Division of Thomas Nelson Publishers
Since 1798

visit us at www.westbowpress.com

Published in Nashville, Tennessee, by WestBow Press, a division of
Thomas Nelson, Inc.

Publisher's Note: This novel is a work of fiction. Names, characters,
places, and incidents are either products of the author's imagination
or used fictitiously. All characters are fictional, and any similarity to
people living or dead is purely coincidental.

Scripture quotations are from the New King James Version,
copyright © 1982 by Thomas Nelson, Inc.

Grateful acknowledgement is made for permission to reprint the
following: "Live Like You Were Dying" by Tim Nichols and Craig
Wiseman, copyright © 2003 Warner-Tamerlane Publishing Corp.
and Big Loud Shirt Industries. All Rights Reserved. Used by
Permission. Warner Bros. Publications U.S. Inc., Miami, Florida
33014

Library of Congress Cataloging-in-Publication Data

CIP Applied For

Printed in the United States of America

04 05 06 07 08 QW 6 5 4 3 2 1

For my dad—Larry Stroud—
a man who has always been man enough
to say, "I love you."

Acknowledgments

Prior to learning that Westbow Press wanted to publish a novel based on "Live Like You Were Dying," I had heard the song on the radio and instantly pictured the character that grew to become Nathan. Thank you, Craig Wiseman and Tim Nichols, for writing a beautiful song that inspires and challenges on so many different levels.

I'm also grateful to Jenny Baumgartner and Allen Arnold at Westbow Press for thinking of me for this project. Writing the story was a privilege and has given me pause to rethink my own life.

If it had not been for the kindness of JoAnn Miller in opening up her North Carolina mountain home, the manuscript might not have arrived on schedule. JoAnn, your hospitality and friendship are valued. I also appreciate the friendship and guidance I've received from Dr. Michael Ledet of Mobile, Alabama. Mike, thank you for answering all of my questions with genuine interest in the story.

As always, I'm indebted for the love and support that I continue to receive from my wife, Melanie. To my parents, Larry and Elaine Stroud, thank you for all of your encouragement and advice during the writing of this novel. And finally to my agent and friend, Laurie Liss, thanks for your tireless advocacy and endless humor.

Foreword

This song has clearly taken on a life of its own. I can see it in the reaction of the fans when we play it at our concerts. I can see it in the letters and emails we get from them about how this song has impacted their lives—or made them stop and take stock of their own. I'm blessed to have found this song and I'm blessed with such great fans. But more than that, I'm blessed in my life by my family and friends.

A lot of people assume that I recorded "Live Like You Were Dying" because of the passing of my father, Tug McGraw. But my passion goes a lot further. I love this song because I believe that everyone who hears it will have their own unique reaction to it. Each person has his or her own definition of what it means to "live like you were dying." That's what makes it such a great song.

It's not just about my personal connection—although obviously there is one—it's about how you connect to it. I hope it can provide inspiration for all of us to stop and take time to appreciate all the blessings in our lives—from the smallest things to the biggest dreams. God bless.

Tim McGraw

"Live Like You Were Dying"

by Craig Wiseman and Tim Nichols

He said I was in my early forties
With a lot of life before me
When a moment came that stopped me on a dime
And I spent most of the next days
Looking at the x-rays
And talking 'bout the options, talking 'bout sweet time

And I asked him when it sank in
That this might really be the end
How's it hit ya' when you get that kind of news
Man, what'd you do (he said)

CHORUS
I went sky diving I went rocky mountain climbing
I went two point seven seconds on a bull named Fumanchu
And I loved deeper and I spoke sweeter
And I gave forgiveness I'd been denying
And he said one day I hope you get a chance
To live like you were dying

He said I was finally the husband

That most the time I wasn't

And I became a friend a friend would like to have

And all 'a sudden going fishin'

Wasn't such an imposition

And I went three times that year I lost my dad

And I finally read the good book

And I took a good long hard look

At what I'd do if I could do it all again . . . and then

CHORUS

Like tomorrow was a gift

And you've got eternity to think of what you did with it

What you did with it . . . what did I do with it

CHORUS

Chapter One

A shrill whistle signaling the start of the night shift at the paper mill caused the walls of my office trailer to rattle. Standing at the window, I watched as smoke poured from the tall pipes that lined the top of the plant and twirled up into the dark Georgia sky. The smell of the mill overpowered that of the lukewarm coffee I was drinking, an odor that had almost made me sick the first time I experienced it. "The smell of money," my old college buddy, Jay Beckett, said of the stench that could cause even the hardest of men to curl his nose. When I dropped out of college to work for his start-up company, Beckett Construction, my wife's father had told me that I'd never make more than a laborer's wages. In just twenty years, I was making twice what my father-in-law did and now carried the title of project engineer on a business card. Sweat and long hours had paved the way for success, but the toll I'd paid could not be measured in dollars and cents.

The smell of money turned out to be an axis between my soul and my family. A dividing line that separated me into two halves until I stumbled through life feeling like the magician's assistant in a show I'd once seen.

At a resort theater in the Bahamas, I occasionally glanced at the engineers I was asked to entertain for the sake of renewing a company contract. While the magician with the red cape and black spandex pants guided a chain saw down the center of a white box, the assistant who lay inside never flinched. She just smiled and looked up at the ceiling that glowed with colored lights, withdrawn from the massacre that was taking place below.

While the tips of the assistant's sequined shoes sparkled, the engineers who sat next to me grimaced and sucked in their breath at the idea of the beautiful woman being ripped in two. But I just kept staring at her blue eyes and thinking that I knew how she felt, being torn away bit by bit from a part of your being. That night marked the first time that I'd missed an event in my daughter's life. The night she had walked across the stage at the local community center, looked at her teacher, and reached up her tiny hand for her kindergarten diploma.

Regret was a heavy opponent back then. I flew back to Atlanta crumpled against the plane window, feeling the weight that comes with bad decisions. But over time the trappings of more contracts and larger bonus payouts had tipped the scales of balance. Soon regret was nothing more than a feeling, a slight irritation that could be swatted away with the justification that I was missing family events in order to make those I loved happy with gifts that time could not buy. The rationale never had made any sense to my wife, Heather, no matter how many different ways I tried to explain it or how many times I called to say that I was sorry.

Seven years later I found myself answering my office phone and still offering the same explanations. This one was for my daughter's gymnastic event that I'd missed because of an employee who hadn't bothered to show up for work, but Heather was no longer listening. She was only talking, louder and louder, till I had to pull the phone away from my ear. Even from a distance her question cut through the cloud of excuses and left me remembering exactly how cold the airplane window felt against my face the night I leaned against it and tried to convince myself that work was more important than a kindergarten graduation.

Through the phone line my wife's question sounded like a riddle, but there wasn't any sign of playfulness in the tone. "Tell me something . . . are you just living to work, or working to live?"

A loud noise from the paper mill's compressor broke

the silence, and my metal desk vibrated. At first I thought of acting like I hadn't heard her question. But Heather knew all of my tricks. Ignoring a question might work with my employees, but it never worked with Heather.

"What?" I finally asked.

"You heard me . . . Look, there's no use going over this for the hundredth time. What's done is done. Just promise me that you'll take a nap or something. There's got to be a place you can hole up in for at least thirty minutes. Working a straight double shift, three times in one week . . . missing Malley's gym meet. Come on, Nathan. It's insane."

"Yeah, tell that to the millwright who didn't show up for work tonight. 'A death in the family,' he said. Funny, they always manage to pull off a death when they need to."

"If you don't get some rest, you're going to end up dead from a heart attack or something. Look, we both know that you really don't have to work these hours anymore."

When I exhaled, I tried to cover the phone receiver. "It's shutdown. You know what it's like when it's shutdown. Repairs to the plant have to get done in a short amount of time. Time's money around here. When the plant's not running, nobody's making money, and when nobody's making money, nobody's happy."

When Heather sighed, she didn't bother to try to hide it.

Her breath came through the phone line heavy and aggravated. I pictured her running her hands through the brunette corkscrew curls that bounced around her face and twirling the phone cord tighter around her wrist. "Whatever . . . just promise me that you'll get some rest. A little rest . . . a catnap . . . okay? I worry about you."

Shuffling through the soiled and wrinkled blueprints that draped over the metal desk, I accepted her plea without any resistance. We'd known each other for half of our forty-one years, but there was also so much she couldn't understand.

Before I hung up the phone, the trailer door swung open. A short young man with deep-set eyes, whose name was long lost among the sea of W-2 forms stacked on a card table next to my desk, motioned with his chin toward the plant yard outside. "We got a break to the rupture disk up on tower fourteen."

"You think you can handle changing it?" I asked and reached for the hard hat that hung on a rack behind the file cabinet. If only Heather was still on the phone, she could hear for herself why I had to stay at the job site.

The young man nodded. "Oh, yeah. I just need some backup. The thing is, Kyle didn't show up tonight . . . something about a funeral . . ."

"Yeah, I know all about Kyle," I said, never looking to gauge the young man's reaction.

Outside in the plant yard, rusted pipes and sparks from welding machines littered the concrete floor as men carrying buckets of tools made their way past us. Beyond the plant gates, the interstate hummed with traffic. Bright light from the plant spotlights rained down on us as though we were celebrities at a fancy black-tie event. But the only black ties were those made of grease and dirt, woven permanently into the shirts of the men and women who kept a steady stream of money flowing for the mill owners.

Climbing the ladder to the sixty-foot tower, I watched as the boy who was trying to be a man paused halfway up. "You okay up there?" I yelled.

He never looked back before climbing another few feet. It would be a cat-and-mouse game that continued for the length of our journey. If the millwright had shown up for work, I wouldn't be out here. The thought kept playing in my mind, stirring up the anger that caused me to climb faster until I was inches from the young man and the hardened clay that lined the soles of his work boots. "Am I fixing to have to light a match under you? I don't want to be up here till sunrise."

At the top of the tower, the crisp, early-March wind

clipped against my face, and off in the distance, the high-rise buildings of downtown Atlanta sparkled. Hissing steam rose from the dome-shaped tower that held the disk. I motioned for the young assistant to put the tools on the floor of the catwalk.

If it hadn't been for the risk of releasing chlorine dioxide into the plant, I most likely would have told him to save the job for the morning crew. Turning to ask for the wrench, I found the young assistant holding on to the rail of the cat-walk that circled the tower. Sweat trickled down the side of his stubbled face, which was growing paler by the second. "You gonna make it?" I called out.

He never looked away from the top of the tower that loomed ten more feet above us. At first he nodded and then shook his head. "The stairs got to me. I'm feeling . . . something's not right with my stomach."

Fishing through the box of tools he managed to place on the catwalk floor, I looked down at workers the size of ants. They scurried about the plant just like it was their own personal anthill. "You're not scared of heights, now, are you?" I yelled to the young man.

"No . . . but Kyle usually takes care of this."

"Yeah," I said. "Well, Kyle ain't here tonight." Part of me wanted to chew him out for not telling me in the first place that he was too yellow-bellied to do the job, but the other part of me wanted to laugh. "I tell you what," I said, strapping the gas mask around my neck. "You stand over there, glued to that rail, and when I lean down and hand you the old disk, you just lean out and hand me the new one. Sound like a plan?" The entire moment summed up my basic philosophy on life: if you want something done right, you have to do it yourself.

As I climbed up the ten-foot ladder, the tower hissed like it was ready for a fight. I paused long enough to look out across the rows of pipes that created the plant's skyline. The bright spotlights overpowered the darkness, and even from a respectable distance, the heat from the lights singed my neck as good as any tanning bed that my twelve-year-old daughter argues that she is old enough to visit.

With the mask now in place and the rust-stained wrench in hand, I went to work. Three bolts came off of the old, cracked disk with ease. Then something scratched against my leg, throwing me off balance. My breath was heavy and echoed against the vinyl mask that fogged with each word I yelled. "Wait a minute. I'm still trying to get the bolt off of this one. Give me the new one when I motion for you." The assistant was reaching upward, holding the disk as if it was a gift for his daddy. His face contorted in either strain or confusion, he stared up at me and lifted the replacement disk even higher.

When I turned back to the stubborn bolt, the white beam shining from the spotlight across the way blinded my vision. For a second I only saw black and then hazy shapes of gray. Out of instinct or fear, I reached out, trying to find the bolt with the wrench. Heat from the disk scalded the tips of my gloved fingers as I struggled to make out the shape of the bolt. "Got it!" I yelled, but the sound never left the inside of the mask.

The thrill of the catch would be the last thing I remembered that night. When I yanked the bolt free with the wrench, my foot slipped from the ladder and the wrench fell faster than I did. No childhood scenes flashed before my eyes. There were only sounds. Yells from the young assistant, clanging from the scattered tools on the catwalk, and the hissing of the tower above me—sounds that rang in my ears until the pain made me scream out.

When I hit the safety rail on the catwalk chest-first, I flipped before landing on the platform floor. My body twisted with pain until breathing became the hardest job I'd ever faced. Even the ammonia scent of the paper mill, that smell of money, couldn't wake me from the darkness that settled over me.

Chapter Two

"You're going to be okay. Everything's okay now." My wife repeated the words so many times that at first I thought they were lyrics to a song I'd heard long ago but had since forgotten. Her words mingled with the sound of the electrical pump that forced my lungs to operate. The first thing I felt was the soreness in my throat, a pain that caused me to think someone had scraped the inside of my mouth with a razor blade. When I opened my eyes, I fought a burning sting until I was finally able to focus and find her.

Standing over me, Heather's face seemed to glow. Her dark eyes were as wild as they had been when we used to sit in the back of my truck and count the stars that held court over her daddy's fishing pond. The bright light behind her head caused her olive skin to seem like it had been painted with milk. Curls of her hair fell free from the clip that was holding it together. She smiled as a tear fell from her eye to my face. "Don't you do that again. Don't you scare me that way," she whispered and made a weak attempt to laugh.

A nurse in a white jacket appeared from behind a curtain, and I saw a beige-colored machine attached to the tube that snaked into my mouth. The woman smiled and nodded at Heather. "He's coming around the bend now."

My words were slow in forming and fought against the tube that filled my throat. Heather placed her hand lightly against my arm. "You were in a fall at the mill," she said in a slow, steady pace. "You had blood in your lungs. Your whole right side was just solid-white on the X-ray. They had to go in and put in a chest tube . . . but don't worry about all that now. You just rest. Don't try to talk. Just rest. There will be plenty of time for talking."

I tried to lift my hand to brush the hair from the side of her face. It was my wife's face that I wanted to see now more than ever. But the darkness wouldn't let me.

———

Lucky, survivor, blessed—these were just a few of the words that people used to describe my experience. A parade of doctors offered words like *tamponade* and other hogwash-sounding terms to describe what had happened to me. "Blood on the lungs" remained the easiest way to understand how close I'd come to cheating death. A few more minutes of waiting for the paramedics, and most likely I'd have drowned in my own blood.

When I came off the ventilator three days later, I was

moved to a private room. A nurse with pink lipstick painted over thin lips delivered cards from family back in my hometown of Choctaw, Georgia. Here, though, only the teachers who worked with Heather—and one next-door neighbor—took notice of my accident. That's when I started realizing how few people in this big city knew me.

My grandmother, Grand Vestal, sent a card covered in wildflowers that she had painted herself, using the flowers that grew in her pasture as inspiration. She signed the card from both her and my father. Even though my father was her son-in-law, she took care of the emotional side of his business just like my mother always had.

"I couldn't get satisfied until I heard your voice," my grandmother said through the phone that Heather held up to my ear. Her words hazed my mind until all I could picture were the gray braided pigtails that hung low around her shoulders and the way her earth-stained face would tighten whenever she was concerned. My grandmother was the keeper of my childhood memories, of days spent learning how to reap food from the soil that had first belonged to her Creek Indian people.

"Don't worry about me, Grand Vestal. I'm okay, really," I said, trying to sound as lighthearted as possible. But something wouldn't let me believe that everything would be okay. Carefree days at my grandmother's were tucked too far away in the back of my mind. Time and responsibilities had shoved them inside a vault whose combination I no longer seemed to know. Now the projects that I'd left behind at the paper mill hindered me as much as the bandages around my chest.

Jay Beckett and the rest of the gang from the construction company sent over a fruit basket that filled every inch of the portable tray table. "We can't have this now," the pink-lipsticked nurse said as she moved the basket from where the delivery person had placed it, clucking her tongue like a disapproving mother hen. "We need to keep gifts off of this table. We have to keep a place for our meals, don't we?" By the second day, her use of the word *we* wore my nerves down to the quick.

But the day that I was able to sit up in bed, the real gift that I'd been waiting for arrived. My daughter, Malley, stood in front of Heather with her arms folded across her stomach, only moving them once to push the auburn hair from her eyes. Her eyes were as green as my own, and every time I looked into them, I saw the best part of me. Heather nudged her forward slightly, but it was only when I reached out my arm to Malley that she locked ahold of me until my chest ached. I could only imagine what it must have been like for my twelve-year-old baby to toy with the idea of losing her daddy. Holding her and feeling the beat of her heart against my own, I could only relate by knowing how painful it was to watch my own mama die of pancreatic cancer two years before. I guess whether you're twelve or thirty-nine, the pain and fear that come with loss sting just the same.

When my family doctor came in carrying my ever-growing medical file, Malley was sitting in the chair beside me. We'd been playing a match on the new electronic tennis game that she had bought. A man no older than myself, the doctor had a soul better suited for a man my father's age. His smile was slanted and his eyes tired.

"When am I going to be able to check out?" I asked. "Did you know that there are 427 specks on that ceiling tile? Now, that shows you how bad this place is wearing on me."

The doctor rubbed his chin and looked at Heather. "He's back kicking, I see."

Heather laughed and winked at Malley. "Now you see why we want him to stay in here as long as possible."

It hurt when I laughed, so I held it in and felt the blood rush to my face. Malley laughed harder and pointed at me. "Look at him. He's getting bashful."

As soon as the laughter faded, the doctor rose up on his toes and coughed. "No, we'll have you out of here in no time. First I want you to have another X-ray. You know, to make sure you're all clear of the blood. For once it'll be a relief just to see three cracked ribs."

———

Relief never came. The same doctor now stood over me, pointing to the new X-rays on the lighted screen behind my hospital bed. I could only hear his words and watch Heather's reaction as she gripped her necklace tighter. "It's just happenstance that we found it," the doctor said. A single white spot remained on the screen.

"A smudge," I first suggested, but all Heather did was look down and offer a smile as tight as the nurse who cared for me. Later I studied the X-rays on my own and gazed at the foreign white object on the lung pocket outlined before me. While the doctor talked of specialists and second opinions, I stared at the spot, trying to will it away, to force the smudge from the screen and away from my life.

This isn't me, I kept thinking. During hunting season I can outrace a fox and stay squatting in a tree stand for hours on end without even a single muscle cramping. I can climb sixty-foot towers at work and never lose my breath. The smudge on the black celluloid had to be nothing more than somebody's fingerprint. A mistake most likely caused when the X-ray was processed. "Sugar Boy, just dismiss it from your mind with a good old belly laugh," I heard my grandmother call out from the brightest corners of my mind. Her mind-over-matter techniques had been freely dispensed throughout the years. Time and time again her wisdom reigned over any advice I'd ever gotten from a licensed doctor. Even so, my mind couldn't talk my fingers out of lightly touching the thick bandages, the place of shelter for the white smudge that they claimed lived within me. I fought the image of the smudge setting up camp inside my lung. Shooing away the feeling of depression, I forced myself to follow my grandmother's prescription.

On my last night in the hospital, I stared out my window at the parking-lot lights, shining down like imitation stars. The real stars were what I longed to see. Self-pity swarmed around my room. Swatting back, I could almost hear Grand Vestal's raspy voice reminding me that laughter is the best medicine for a troubled soul. So when the dinner tray was placed before me, I prepared the ingredients for my home remedy.

———

An hour later, a nurse's aid entered. "You didn't eat your food," she said and noted something on a card.

"No ma'am, I think I'll just keep this apple juice. I might get thirsty later in the night."

The next morning I placed the unopened container of apple juice under the sheets. The nurse with the pink lipstick entered the room with her usual singsong welcome. "And how are we doing this morning? Did we have a restful night?" She asked the questions without so much as looking up from her clipboard.

"Awful," I replied.

"Well, that's nice. We need our rest. Now, you know the routine: it's sample time," she said, shaking the plastic cup in the air. "Do we need help getting to the bathroom this morning?"

I never answered but instead shook my head, if only to make her look up from the clipboard. "Now, are you sure? We wouldn't want a fall."

Nodding, I smiled, and she managed to smile too, albeit a forced one. "Well, if we start feeling lightheaded, just pull on the safety string in the bathroom. I'll be right outside the door."

After she left I opened the container of apple juice and poured it into the sample container. The nurse came back into the room wearing plastic gloves and carrying a red marker. Before she could remove the container from the tray table, I touched the side of my head and moaned.

"Are we having some pain? On a scale of one to ten, rate it."

"No, I just . . . I think I got sort of woozy using the bathroom. Everything started spinning around, and my mouth got all dry."

The nurse clucked her tongue and leaned down closer. The pen attached to a string around her neck swung in circles.

"Where am I?" I asked in a half-voice, half-moan sort of way.

She clapped her hands close to my face and then moved closer until the smell of her hairspray almost overpowered me. "We're in the hospital. Now, do we know our name?"

"Thirsty," I moaned.

"What? Speak up."

"Thirsty," I said again.

Before she could move completely away from me, I snatched the sample container from the tray table and gulped it down right in front of her.

By now she was literally having a running fit, jogging in place and waving her hands. "No, no!" she said in a high-pitched screech. "No, no . . . That's our . . . that's our sample." Openmouthed, she looked around the room, as if a security camera might have captured her momentary lack of control, and then fled from the room faster than I ever thought she could move.

Leaning against the pillows, I laughed an old-fashioned howl and ignored the pain. For the first time since being admitted to the hospital, I finally felt stronger than the fear of the unknown.

Chapter Three

After seven days of what felt like hard time, I was released from the hospital. I'd never been so grateful for anything in all my life.

"Daisies," I said, pointing to a bunch of wildflowers growing around a stop sign near the entrance of our neighborhood.

"What?" Heather asked, leaning over the car console, closer to me.

"I never noticed those daisies before," I said.

Turning the car to the shoulder of the road, she got out and plucked two of the flowers. Back inside, she handed them to me. "What did you do that for?"

"Because I felt like it," she said and continued driving. "Two flowers to remind you that you've got two people who love you more than you know."

At home Malley had made a sign that spelled out "Welcome Home" in gold stars. "Do you know how many boxes of stars it took me to make that sign?"

Right then I knew something had changed. Looking down at the scattered pieces of adhesive paper that were left from Malley's workmanship, I never once mentioned that she needed to clean up the mess. I guess the difference was, now I chose not to speak the words, even if they ran through my mind. "How 'bout two daisies for payment? To remind you that you have your mama and me to love you."

As Malley twined the flowers together into a bracelet, I sat on the leather sofa that I'd bought for Heather the Christmas before last. "Did anybody from work call here today?"

"No, were you expecting them to?" Heather asked from the kitchen. The sound of water being poured into a pot rang out into the living room.

"Just wondering," I mumbled. Curious to know if the guys all showed up for work without me there, I toyed with the idea of trying to drive to the job site but gave up on the idea, knowing how bad Heather would throw a fit. How many had taken sick days? Were we still on schedule? The questions swirled around in my head until I gripped the edge of the sofa cushion, fighting to keep myself from picking up the phone.

———

After dropping Malley off at school, Heather and I fought the rush-hour traffic into town. Sitting in bumper-to-bumper traffic, we inched closer to the skyline and the approaching exit for Emory University Hospital. The tall buildings seemed bigger than usual, and I pictured them squeezing up against us, pushing out all the air until breathing was something I had to work at doing. Never letting on to Heather, I kept a steady drumbeat with the music that played on the radio. With each tap of my finger against the car door, I pictured the anxiety being knocked out of my system and rolling underneath the tires of our car.

At the hospital we sat in the lung specialist's office, listening as the ticking of a steel clock competed with the humming of an air vent. Certificates lined one wall, while the clock and a painting of a woman stared out from the other side of the office. The surgeon who had advised me to have the mass cut out had directed us to this doctor whose last name was as long as the degrees that framed his wall. They all claimed that this man was the best lung specialist in the South, if not the whole country.

When he walked into the office, he smiled warmly and patted the copies of my X-rays that he carried alongside a file stamped with my name. He was an older man with a row of sparse hair that circled his bald crown like spring grass around the edges of a freshly tilled field. Tapping a gold pen against his desk, the doctor looked at me and shook his head.

"The conventional side of me tends to agree with what the surgeon told you." The doctor raised his arm in the air like he was fighting a war. "Let's get on with it and take this mass out." His words rolled over us and he chuckled before shaking his head again. "But the side of me that's been treating patients for thirty-two years says to hold off, to wait awhile."

"What about this thing inside of him? You're telling us to just ignore it?" Heather was leaning closer to the edge of her seat and licking her lips, ready to pounce.

"I never meant 'ignore it.' Monitor perhaps, but not ignore." The doctor rotated the pen between his fingers like it was a minibaton. He smiled and looked straight at me. "Mr. Bishop, I don't pull any punches. Quite frankly, I don't have any left to pull. What your surgeon advised you is conventional thought, but the one thing that I've learned is that convention is worth about a pound of manure. Your lungs have been through a trauma that nearly cost you your life. You're still mending . . . this idea of yet another surgery so soon . . . well . . ."

"What about treatments?" I asked.

"That's a fair question," the doctor said. "But I'm not an

oncologist. I'm a pulmonologist. The best advice I can give you is, whatever action you decide to take should be your call, not a physician's."

"Any other people with cases like mine?"

"I've seen patients who have had similar cases, yes. Some ended up having benign tumors that occur in embryonic tissue, meaning that they've always been there. Others ended up having a malignancy. I guess my question is, how is this X-ray on my desk going to change the outcome?"

"Uh, now, I don't mean any disrespect by saying this, but isn't that why I'm paying you?" I asked.

The doctor tipped the pen toward me and smiled. "No disrespect taken. Better phrased, what if you never had the accident? What if you never knew that you had this mass? What would you be doing differently?"

He made notations in my file but never gave me the opportunity to answer his question. It was a homework type of question, and I studied on it day and night. Try as I might to forget it, the sound of this doctor's voice never left my mind.

———

That night I dreamed that an alien-looking creature the size of one of Malley's old Barbie dolls ripped through my skin and ran away before I could ask it why it had invaded me in the first place. Jolted awake and covered in sweat, I rolled over and groaned. Pain shot through my chest, but I still managed to put my arm around Heather. She and Malley were my world. The spot, whatever it may be, was helping me to realize that more now than ever before.

The morning after my visit with the lung doctor, decisions fit for a four-year-old, such as what cereal to eat in the morning, seemed complicated. What would the spot in my chest want to eat? Would oat bran drive it from my body, or would a hefty batch of sugarcoated nuggets do the trick? I finished a huge bowl of both cereals and heard a car in the driveway. From the kitchen window, I saw Jay Beckett close the door of his black Range Rover.

Jay sat across from me in my easy chair while I fought the pain of sitting upright against the sofa. His wire-rimmed glasses sloped down his slightly crooked nose, and he didn't waste any time by pushing them back up. "So, it's going good, huh?" Jay kept placing the cup of coffee back and forth on the table. Finally, he settled for putting the mug down and leaned over like a defensive center ready to strike.

"Pretty good," I said, nodding in hopes that he would believe the lie.

"I tell you something: the guys down at the mill are

having a time. I mean, a devil of a time trying to get those repairs done on schedule without you."

I knew I would feel it sooner or later, and there it was: guilt. For the past twenty years I'd given heart and soul to that mill, without any memorable vacation to speak of, and after ten days away, I was getting antsy. The mill needed me. Jay stared at me over the top of his glasses, seeming to know exactly what I was thinking.

"Don't you worry about a thing. We want you well . . . yes sir. We take care of our people. You know that."

"I appreciate it," I said. "But that mill project is my baby. You know I want it done right."

"Done right or not done at all," Jay said and tried to laugh. "You remember that one? That's what you said the first time you pitched us to the mill and almost got sick from the smell of the place." Jay laughed and ran his hand through his black hair, now tinged with gray, just as he had the day he convinced me to bypass college for a quicker payout.

"Yeah," I said and reached for my coffee. Circling my finger around the warm edges of the cup, I debated how much more to share with this man who was both friend and boss.

"You say you got another doctor's appointment tomorrow?" Jay asked.

I bit my bottom lip and grimaced, and then, fearing that I might seem weak, I chuckled. "They're working me over, but good. I think they've got a beach house to pay off or something."

"Man, do what you need to do. Listen to the doctors."

"Huh . . . that's just it. They don't tell me much." Laying out the details of the suspicious spot, I watched Jay frown and then shake his head. "What're you going to do?" he asked.

"I'm trying to figure it all out. Day by day, you know."

When he got up to leave, he reached over and patted my arm. "Let's hope that oncologist you're seeing will point you in the right direction."

Watching Jay back out of the driveway, I wanted to run out the door and tell him that it was all a joke to buy me some time off. But it wasn't a joke, and Jay sensed it the same way he could sense a vulnerable competitor ready for the kill.

The next afternoon, Heather and I waited in yet another doctor's office in downtown Atlanta. Various images of my mama during her downward spiral from pancreatic cancer floated through my mind. Treatment after treatment had left my mama a shattered woman with a tumor that refused to be broken. The last time I visited her, she had just had a procedure that was supposed to dry up the cause of her ailments. All it did was speed up her departure from this world. "I haven't felt the same since," she said with chapped and weathered lips. Her chalk-white hands matched the color of the sheet where she lay. "I'm just tired . . . just plain tired." The way she died haunted me as much as her appearance the last time I saw her. She was alone when she left this world. My father had slipped off so that he could catch up on some sleep. In the end he had disappointed her, and the bitterness that I felt toward him had taken root.

The doctor walked through the door and sat across from us at her mahogany desk. She had horn-rimmed glasses and streaks of gray throughout the chestnut hair that she twirled around her finger as she reviewed my chart. "I'm also inclined to say monitor it," she said, putting my file on her desk. "I'd give it another month or two and then return for a follow-up X-ray and CT scan. However . . ." She looked away toward the gray sky beyond her window and then back to my medical file. "If you're inclined not to wait, there is a study that a colleague of mine is leading. It's a trial for an experimental drug that increases the likelihood of . . ." *Experimental* was the only word I needed to hear to know it was time for me to leave. She might as well have put a collar around my neck and called me her pet guinea pig.

"What's the matter?" Heather called out, running behind me in the hall.

I passed a janitor slapping the floor with his wet mop. The elevator was now in full view. Heather hurried toward me, the tips of her heels clipping the floor like a military drumbeat meant for battle. All I could picture was the sight of my mother with cords snaking into her veins, spitting out the liquids that were referred to by code names. Experiments had done my mother in; I was sure of it. Now it was time for me to do what she should have done before her veins became bruised, squiggly lines that looked like worms beneath a layer of thin skin. It was time to break free and run.

Heather never said a word as I slipped into the driver's seat of our car. She knew me well enough to know that driving was something I had to do, something I could still control. We left the parking lot and drove in silence back to the bedroom community that housed Atlanta's businesspeople, a world that I increasingly felt was not my own.

———

Following the doctor's appointment, I couldn't sleep at all. After tossing for half the night, I finally got out of bed at 4:30 and reached for the medicine that had always helped to soothe me in the past: work. I didn't tell Heather I was planning on returning to the mill because I knew that I'd never hear the end of it.

"What in the world are you doing?" she asked, squinting in the harsh bathroom light.

With toothbrush in hand, I rolled my eyes and sighed. "I'm just going in for a little while."

"What?" Her voice was loud and her stance at the door told me that she was not giving in. "It's not even daylight outside." She glanced down at my work boots and threw her hands up in the air. "Unbelievable."

Following her back into the bedroom, I pulled a shirt from the closet and slapped the watch on my wrist.

"You know, the doctor hasn't signed a release for you to return to work yet."

"That hasn't stopped me before now."

Heather yanked the blanket from the bed. "Why are you doing this, Nathan? Did Jay say something the other day?"

"No, Jay said nothing. Look, it's me. I need to work, Heather. If you want me sane, I need to work."

"So this is what you're going to do? You're going to go hide out at the job site every day instead of making a decision about what the doctors said."

I finished buttoning my shirt and flipped off the light switch, hoping that it would turn off the conversation too.

"No sir," Heather said and flipped the light switch back on. "You're not getting away with this. For once, Nathan, think about someone other than yourself."

Her words pounded up against me until my chest ached even more. "What do you mean?"

"I have watched you put that job first so many times that I can't even count them anymore. You've never once thought of the cost to me or Malley."

"What are you talking about? I work like a dog to provide for my family."

"You're talking about things. I'm talking about your presence in this house. You know, it's funny: I thought the one good thing that could come out of your accident was being able to have you around more often. And now, here you are, wanting to run right back to work."

Heather pushed me away when I tried to hug her. "Don't, Nathan. Don't patronize me. I won't stand here and watch you kill yourself. I refuse." She turned off the light and fell into bed, pulling the sheet up around her neck.

The ticking of the hallway clock let me know that time had not stood frozen. I eased out of the bedroom and contemplated still going into work, but Heather's words kept me fenced for the time being. Outside, the stars were fading, and a turquoise color was rising up against the dark sky. An early-morning chill snapped me back to life. Heather had never understood why I needed to work harder than most. She had a college degree. My shortcut to the working world ended up being a shortfall for my self-esteem. Success at work was the adrenaline I craved, an assurance that I was not a failure in a world where opinions about men were made based on which engineering school they attended.

A cloud of tension hung over the breakfast table that morning. While Malley cleared the dishes, I rubbed Heather's back, trying to ask forgiveness without coming out and doing so. She nodded a weak acceptance and called out to Malley, "Go get your book bag. I don't want to be late for work."

After they left I poured a cup of strong coffee in my travel mug and headed out for the mill. Heather might be upset if she found out that I went to work, but she'd be a whole lot more upset without a paycheck coming in to cover our mortgage.

When I got there, Rex, the mill gate guard, sheltered his eyes from the morning sun. "Nathan? What in the world are you doing here?"

"Rex, they're working me over, but good," I said, just as I had since the day we took on the mill project.

"They told me you wouldn't be back here for another three months or more," Rex said and scribbled something on his clipboard.

"Well, they told you wrong." As I started to drive away, Rex's words caused me to brake.

"You're gonna have to park out in the hourly employee area, though."

His cheeks blushed, and he flipped the pages on the clipboard. "A boy named Livingston showed up here last week, and they told me to give him your parking place. He don't look to be more than nineteen, if you ask me."

Driving through the mill, explanations for the situation flooded my mind. Most likely Livingston, the boy who'd just graduated from Georgia Tech's engineering school, was filling in to make sure the shutdown project went according to plan. Besides, he had his own project at the textile mill in LaGrange to worry with.

Walking through the employee parking lot, I saw the boy wonder's Jeep parked in my spot right next to the metal trailer. Inside, the parts-supply man, Riley, was fixing a new pot of coffee. He flinched when he saw me walk in.

"Well, hey . . . didn't expect to see you."

"I got tired of counting ceiling tiles."

Riley stepped in front of me, still holding the can of Folger's. "Everybody's back there having a meeting in your office."

"Yeah, who's everybody?"

He glanced back at my office door and moved to let me slide past the copy machine. There were roughly twenty steps from the copier to my office door, but the voices floating from beneath the door made it seem more like two miles. Explanations that I had dreamed up while driving to the parking lot crumbled when I opened the door and found Brad Livingston sitting in my chair with his boots propped up on the desk. His eyes widened, and when he moved his feet, a set of plans fell to the floor. All of the foremen that I'd hired stood and tried to smile as if they'd expected me.

"Looks like I'm interrupting something."

"No, that's quite all right," Brad said, rising to reach out his hand. "We're just having our weekly update."

"How you making it these days?" Cal Rufford, the foreman over welders, asked.

"Cal, I'm back to normal. Yeah, I woke up this morning thinking about that vat drum project that we need to—"

"Uh, Nathan, we finished that last week," Brad said and

tapped his fingers against a stack of blueprints. "Hey, look, we're all adults here. Nathan, why don't you pull up a chair and join us."

Brad's starched blue shirt wrinkled as he folded his arms. I stared at him long enough to make him reach down and fidget with the edge of a file on my desk.

"I guess I lost the memo that said you were taking over my job."

Brad tossed his hands in the air and tried to joke it off. "Hey, with the pressure we're under to get these projects in on time, I'm beginning to wish I hadn't gotten the memo either." Nobody followed Brad's laugh, and he ended up coughing.

Cal was looking down, tapping his pencil against a spiral notepad. "Is this the way it is, Cal? Have they replaced me with Super Boy?"

"Nathan, there's no need for that," Brad answered for Cal. "We're all on the same team here, and—"

"Yeah," Cal interrupted. "That's more or less what happened."

"Cal, let's not get into HR matters," said Brad. "Look, Nathan, we welcome you here anytime. Jay has assured me that you'll always have a place at Beckett Construction. Hey, if you were up to it, I could slot you as a millwright today."

"A millwright?"

A shrill whistle from the plant vibrated the trailer, and the loudness washed away any words that might have been spoken.

Walking past the copier, I tried to smile at Riley, just to let him know that the general was not fading into the sunset, but he never looked up. He just continued counting the number of bolts that were inside a plastic box.

During the drive from the mill, I cussed that freckle-faced boy who had begged me with everything he was worth to leave college to work with him. Blood boiled until my hands twitched from pure hatred for Jay Beckett. My truck had practically memorized the drive to the corporate office, and I never even recalled taking the exit off of the interstate.

Located on the fourteenth floor of rented office space, Jay prided himself on being able to look out of his floor-to-ceiling office windows and see Stone Mountain. Now it was my plan to let him take a flight to the mountain by personally throwing him out the window.

When I opened the glass doors to the office, a young temporary worker with a row of pierced earrings scanned me from head to toe.

"Get Jay Beckett out here," I demanded.

She knocked over the trash basket while trying to move away from the desk. After she had disappeared down the hall, Louise Finches walked out into the lobby, shaking her head. An older woman with bouffant red hair and a no-nonsense style, she had been with the company as long as I had. As the office manager, she knew Jay as good as anybody, and probably better than his wife.

She glanced at the young receptionist. "I'll take it from here." She swept the air with her hands, and the young woman darted away.

"Louise, now, don't get in the middle of this. This is between Jay and me."

"Honey, I know, but he's not here today."

Pacing around the glass coffee table that was most likely a rental, I never paused when a magazine fell to the floor. "Don't start, Louise. Don't patronize me like this. He's here and I know it."

"Now, Nathan, get ahold of yourself." Louise gripped my shoulders and looked me square in the eye. Her dark eyes were tired and circled in loose skin. "You've got a wife and a daughter to think about. Go home and take care of them. Take care of yourself. Come back after your body has healed. This isn't nothing but a thing. Just a job, for crying out loud."

I laughed and then became concerned when my voice cracked. This place was not a job to me. It was my *life*. I had worked my tail to the bone for this business, and now they were pushing me out.

Two women leaned against the frosted glass wall that separated the reception area from the rest of the office. When I glanced in their direction, they flinched and walked away.

"Here's the problem with you boys," Louise went on. "You think life is nothing but profits and margins. You of all people should know different. You almost lost your life once already for such foolishness. Take this time off, Nathan. When you're better, then deal with it." She squeezed my shoulders. "Go home. It's where you belong right now."

"Go ahead then; protect him."

"Honey, I'm protecting *you*."

Turning to leave, I yanked the glass door to the office with everything that I had in me. The door crashed against the wall and a gasp rang out. The sound of shattering glass brought the rest of the office staff out into the reception area. Looking over my shoulder, the last thing I saw before I walked into the elevator was Louise standing in the middle of the group, looking at me with her mouth wide open. Glass once painted with the Beckett Construction logo that I had helped design now rested in pieces at her feet.

———

After supper, I sat on the step outside our front door as country as I pleased, wearing only jeans. It was the first time that I had dared to sit out in the yard shirtless and shoeless. The white bandage covering my outward wound shined for all the neighborhood to see, but my inner wound was buried so far down that not even Malley and Heather could detect it.

The smell of freshly cut grass and the squeals of playing children were the only indicators that a change of seasons was taking place. Our brick house was complete with two white columns next to the front door. My hard work, common sense, and long hours had paved our entrance into Atlanta's latest gated subdivision, complete with a community swimming pool. Now the job that had made it all possible was being managed by a boy who was technically young enough to be my son.

When the front door opened, light from the living room fanned across the manicured grass, and the sound of a TV show poured out into the night. Heather squeezed in next to me on the step and hooked her arm into mine. The smell of her skin was as pure as the crisp spring air.

"What're you out here thinking?"

I shrugged and pointed toward the house across from us. "Do you know who lives there?"

She followed my point and then looked back at me. "Well, yeah. Ken and Gloria."

"What's their last name?"

Heather wrinkled her brow and squeezed me slightly as if she thought I might have taken a leave of my senses. "Jarvett, Jarvis . . . something that starts with Jar."

When I laughed, she tossed her head back. "I don't know. What difference does it make?" she asked. "Could be Jarhead for as much as I know."

"That's what I'm getting at. We don't know jack about these people."

"Well, Nathan, we haven't exactly hosted a block party or anything."

"But you know what? In Choctaw we would know them. We'd know their parents, their grandparents."

Heather smiled and rested her hand on her chin. "What's really bothering you tonight? I know it's not knowing the last names of our neighbors."

For a second we just sat there, feeling each other's

breath rise and sink in a pattern that made us seem like we had one heart, one life, and I attempted to ignore her question. "Nothing . . . well, let's just say that you don't have to worry about me going into work, because they don't need me."

"And who cares?" Heather threw her hands up in the air. "Listen to me: *we* need you. We need you right here with us."

A group of children rode past on bicycles, and I thought how much freer I'd felt at that age, with no responsibilities. Heather tapped me on my arm and made me look at her. "When are we going to talk about that doctor we saw yesterday?"

"Seemed nice enough. I didn't like the way she kept playing with her hair, though."

"Don't give me that. You know what I'm talking about. The options."

"Options!" I almost coughed out the word. "Not many of her options sounded too good to me."

"Well, we can always go back to the surgeon and tell him . . ."

Pulling at a loose string at the waist of my jeans, I shook my head. "No, I'm through with their options. That lung doctor is the only one who made a lick of sense. I'm through with discussing, cussing, and discussing this mess yet again."

"So, what are you saying? You're just not going to do anything about it?"

"No, not right now I'm not. I'm going to do like the lung doctor suggested. I'm going to wait until I get better before I go under the knife again. I just want to wait awhile."

"But Nathan . . . we don't know how much time we have to wait."

I leaned forward and clasped her fingers into mine. "You know what I was thinking about the entire way to the doctor's office? I was thinking about Mama. She lived the end of her life scared and chasing potions. And what did it get her? A month or two, maybe? If you ask me, it robbed her of a whole lot more. No, I'm not ready to pay that price just yet."

Heather looked off into the distance, and when she turned back to me her eyes were filled with tears. "I knew that's what you were thinking the second you got up and walked out of that doctor's office."

Squeezing her hand, I felt the pulse of her heart. "What if it's been there since I was born? The doctor said that could be the case. It's not going anywhere."

"Yeah, and what if it hasn't been there that long? What if it's . . ."

"Heather, I'm not going to live like that . . . I won't live by what-ifs."

She nodded and looked up at the fading sky as if she might could find the right words to say. Wiping away her tears, I kissed her right in front of God and everybody on our manicured street. Heather wrapped her arms around my neck and rested her head against my shoulder as she had when we were just kids dating back in Choctaw, Georgia.

My real life, the life I'd meant to live all along, was just beginning, and somewhere in the back of my mind I memorized the date of that day, the same as I would the birthday of someone I loved.

Chapter Four

The next morning, after Malley and Heather left for the day, I washed the dishes and cleaned up the kitchen. I struggled trying to find where everything went. That's the problem with being a stranger in your own kitchen. I had no idea what I would do for the rest of the day. It felt like I hadn't been home in years, and I had to learn how to fit back in. Wiping down the table, I stopped to move a project Malley was working on for school: *The Places I Want to Visit.* I sat down and read through some of her entries: Big Ben, The Leaning Tower of Pisa, The Arc d'Triumphe. Further down on the list she had written the American Girl store, wherever that was, and Six Flags. I held the paper in my hand. Had I not taken my own daughter to Six Flags? Next on the list she'd written The Retro Club in Atlanta. What in the world was The Retro Club? I propped my feet up on the table and read through the list again and again. Reaching for a piece of notebook paper and a pen, I decided to do a little homework of my own. The first thing I would do with my time was to make a list of the places that *I'd* always wanted to visit, remote places I'd seen as a boy in the pages of *National Geographic*.

I struggled to come up with a location to put next to the number one spot on the paper. The practical side of me kept getting in the way. Where would we get the money? Even if I had the money, which place would I want to visit first? I wrote something down but then scratched it out. I wrote another spot down but scratched that out too. The thought of going anywhere other than our yearly trip to Destin seemed insane. We would have to wait until school let out, anyway. But beneath the surface of the excuses, what really fueled the procrastination was anger against Jay Beckett. Even though I understood the pressure of the business world as good as anybody, friendship and loyalty ought to count for something.

———

About an hour before Heather and Malley were scheduled to arrive home, I decided to venture into another place that I had not traveled very often. Opening up the pantry door, I saw spaghetti sauce and boxes of pasta. Heather had always said that I never appreciated the time she took to cook and that I thought our food magically appeared on the table. Now it was time to learn her tricks.

Besides, I wanted to do it for Malley too. She fancied spaghetti the way most people appreciate fresh lobster.

Finding where the pots were kept was my first challenge. Finally I settled for the big copper pot that looked like it could be used for washing a load of clothes. I filled it with water, then looked into the box of needle-thin spaghetti. One box didn't seem nearly enough for a family of three, so I emptied one more box into the boiling water. After putting the sauce on, I stepped back and admired the pots on the stove. That wasn't too tough.

A phone call from my insurance agent took only a few minutes, but the sauce that was cooking in the skillet wouldn't wait. The pan shook and hissed with the scorched smell of burning sauce. When I tried to wipe up the spattered sauce from the edge of the stove, the end of the dishrag touched against the burner and caught fire. I flung the rag into the sink just as the pot of spaghetti boiled over. By the time I put the flame out, the spaghetti had mutated into mounds, filling up every inch of the pot, and even erupting over the edges and onto the kitchen counter and floor.

Determined not to let Heather come home and find my mess, I pulled out a roll of paper towels from the pantry and placed them on the floor like skis. My ribs hurt if I bent over for more than a few minutes, so I drug the paper towels with my feet until every last drop of water and sauce were off the floor. Picking up the towels with my toes, I released them into the trash as well as any trained circus monkey.

By the time Heather and Malley made it home, most of the scorched smell had left the room through the open windows. Spraying a can of deodorant all over the kitchen had helped too.

Malley tossed her book bag to the corner and peeked into the pot. "Did you make this?"

"Sure did," I said, standing in front of the refrigerator and hoping that they wouldn't open it to find the bowls of spaghetti that lined the shelves and inside door. "Don't look so surprised. There's a lot of stuff that you don't know I can do."

———

After supper, I gladly took Heather up on her suggestion to rest and slumped down on the couch with the TV remote. It took a lot of energy to be Chef Boyardee. I didn't know how Heather did it every day.

"What's this?" Malley asked, holding the notebook paper printed with my block letters: THE PLACES I WANT TO VISIT.

"Where'd you get that from?" I tried to raise up from the couch, but pain shoved me back.

"It was on the kitchen counter," Malley said, looking back at the paper. "Are you copying my homework?" I tried to reach for the paper again, but she pulled it away. "You didn't get very far."

"Yeah, well, it's silly."

"What's silly?"

"That list. You caught me building air castles." I smiled, but Malley's frown never disappeared. She looked back at the paper and stared so long that you'd think I had listed a book's worth of places to visit.

"Okay, where do you want to go?" She sat on the floor next to the sofa, strands of her auburn hair tickling against the shin of my leg.

"I don't know. Places I've never been to. Places I'd like to see again."

Malley reached for a pen from the coffee table. "Okay, name one place more than any other place in the whole world that you want to see."

"Any place?" Knowing that my baby girl was going to hold my feet to the fire, I felt like I was signing the answer in blood. The last thing I wanted was for her to think that goals weren't attainable. "Well, let's see, now . . . Holster's Drive-In."

Malley turned and squinted. "What?"

"The Holster Drive-in. It's where your mama and me used to hang out back in high school. The best chili dogs you ever put in your mouth."

"But Daddy, wait a minute . . . we got Hawaii, we got Paris . . ."

"But none of those places have Holster's chili dogs. Put it down, please, and while you're at it, put down Brouser's Pond too. The biggest bass I ever caught was there."

Malley laughed when I stretched out my arms. "I'm not lying to you, now," I said. "Did I ever tell you what I used to do when I was a kid?" She smiled and shook her head. "Every year when Grand Vestal used to set out her garden, I'd help her plow. After we were through I'd take off my shoes and run through the dirt going ninety to nothing."

"What?"

"I used to run through that plowed field wide open with the warm dirt tickling the bottom of my feet."

"Why'd you do that?"

Suddenly I felt just as vulnerable as the boy I was remembering. "Grand Vestal always said it was my way of connecting with my past, her people who had first farmed the land."

"Sounds like you were crazy to me." I heard Heather laugh and turned to see her standing in the door of the living room, holding a magazine.

"Grand Vestal, bless her heart. I love her, but she has some outrageous ideas," Heather said.

My grandmother claimed that laughter was the cure for a troubled soul, and that night my girls' laughter was just what I needed. Malley sat with her arm pressed against my leg, for the first time soaking in the stories about my growing-up days in the south Georgia town. She had visited so seldom that I'm sure to her the clay dirt roads with umbrellas of three-hundred-year-old oak trees seemed as foreign as anything I'd ever seen in *National Geographic*. Malley leaned against me as I told story after story until I felt homesick for the first time in years.

I reached for the paper in Malley's hand, and at the very top of the list, right above the number one spot, I wrote in all capital letters: CHOCTAW, GEORGIA, USA! Malley tacked my wish list to the pink bulletin board in her bedroom. A furry blue tack kept the paper hanging at an angle, next to a handful of crumpled concert tickets.

Later in the night, while the motor of the ceiling fan in our bedroom hummed, I wrapped my ankle around my sleeping wife's foot. Heather had always managed the details of the household, paid the bills, and kept Malley happy and secure. Where had I been during all of those times, like when birthday parties were planned? Sure, I'd

show up and give the courtesy hug, but as far as knowing what was going to be given to our daughter, I'd
always left those details to Heather. I didn't even know
the girls who showed up at the parties. The truth of the
matter was, I'd been paying more attention to the names
on Beckett Construction's payroll than the names my
daughter talked about at the supper table. Now, staring
up at the ceiling fan that clipped away the seconds of the
night, I found myself wanting to know everything about
my daughter.

———

It was four weeks after the accident and the last week
of school before summer break. I dropped Malley off at the
front of the school and saw Deana Trusville in the car
behind me. She was slowly rolling along in her Volvo station wagon, like all the other moms that morning. My
truck with the tinted windows and the metal toolbox in
the back rolled right along with the best of them.

A big-hipped crossing guard wearing patent leather
shoes and a pair of black pants one size too small blew her
whistle and kept the congestion orderly. Just when I
approached the double white lines where children were
walking with book bags that seemed twice as big as them,

I made a jump for it. Getting out of my truck, I walked back to Deana's car.

She seemed startled as her blue eyes searched me and a crease formed in the space above her pointy nose. Cracking the window and looking back at the traffic guard, she just nodded for me to get on with it.

"Hey, I'm Nathan Bishop. You probably don't remember me, but your husband was the engineer I worked with on that plant expansion last year."

She blinked and gave a smile, albeit an obligatory one for the sake of her husband, if nothing else. "Oh."

"You came with him to the Christmas party my company . . . gave last year. We talked about our daughters."

A shrill whistle rang out and Deana pointed toward her windshield. "Oh yes. Uh, I think the woman wants you to move your truck."

"Seeing how our girls are about the same age . . . I was wondering if you've ever heard of a place called The Retro Club before?"

"Yes, I think . . ."

"Is it a place I could take my daughter and some of her friends without them being embarrassed that I'm there?"

"Yes, I think . . ."

"Sir, you need to move your vehicle," the traffic guard yelled, but I continued to ignore her.

"I want this to be a surprise, and if I ask Malley's mama, then the cat's out of the bag . . . you know what I mean—"

Nodding quicker by the second, Deana interrupted me. "My daughter loves The Retro Club. They have preteen night the last Friday of the month."

Before I could thank her, Deana rolled up the window and pulled down the sunglasses that held back her blond hair. "Appreciate it," I said trying to walk as fast as my ribs would let me.

The crossing guard was shaking her head. "You deaf?" she yelled.

When I pulled up to the white crossing lane, the brightness of the guard's orange safety banner almost blinded me. "Life is good . . . try it sometime," I said smiling. The woman looked at me with the same openmouthed wonder that Louise Finches had the day I jerked the glass door from its hinges. I guess whether you're off the chart by acting ugly or nice, people are shocked just the same.

———

That Friday, after Heather and Malley left, I went to work. At the entrance to our subdivision, I dug up the black-eyed Susans that dotted the edge of the road and put them in a pot that I'd been hiding behind the lawn-mower. Not satisfied that there were enough flowers, I drove farther north to the construction site for a new sub-division. To the right I spotted the unspoiled field that I'd scouted earlier in the week. Gold flowers with the center as dark as Heather's eyes covered an embankment that ran along the ditch next to a barbed-wire fence.

At the high school, I sat in the parking lot and waited until the bell signaling the first break rang. That was the signal that the coast was clear in the classroom. I got the janitor, Isaac, to let me borrow a wheelbarrow. A group of girls stared and then giggled when I said, "Maybe one day you'll have somebody deliver flowers to you in a wheelbarrow."

Heather was in the teacher's lounge during the class break, just like her next-door teacher had told me. Easing into the classroom, I began arranging the pots of flowers until the room resembled a country field. Black-eyed Susans covered every square inch of Heather's desk and lined the rows between the student desks. On the chalk-board I wrote: *Why did I do it? Because you're an A Plus Wife, Partner and Friend. I love You X Infinity . . .*

At the end of the school day Heather called to thank me.

She called just as the driver of the limousine I had rented for Malley and her friends pulled up to the house.

"Come go with us," I said after I told her about my plan. "We'll swing by and pick you up."

Heather laughed. "No, sometimes a daughter just needs to be a daddy's girl. Go on and have fun."

"You know, I didn't have enough room on the chalkboard to write everything that I wanted to say." I felt like a young kid talking on the phone to his girlfriend.

"And what is that?" she asked.

"Nothing in my life was right until we hooked up," I said, my voice cracking like an adolescent's.

"I know," she whispered. "I know. Well, go on before you're late picking up the girls."

The girls, as in six girls, were all of Malley's closest friends. I had called their parents earlier in the week and made the girls take a vow of secrecy. So far so good. I had told Malley's friends to wait with her by the flagpole. I saw them from the distance and had the driver pull right in front of the flagpole. I watched Malley as the girls started to giggle. She had no idea what was happening.

"Anybody need a ride around here?" I called out while standing through the sunroof.

Malley threw her hand over her mouth. "What's this all

about?" she cried between her fingers as the girls started to pour into the limo.

"This is your night out on the town. Come on. Get in!"

"I swear, if I get embarrassed . . ." Malley said, looking around.

"You'll what?" I asked, jumping out of the car to help her inside. "You'll get embarrassed . . . but what if tonight goes down as one of the best nights of your life? Are you going to remember it?"

She shook her head and laughed. "Daddy, you're so crazy these days."

"Yeah, well, just wait to see how crazy I get tonight," I said, striking a John Travolta dance pose with my finger up in the air and my legs bent far apart.

"Oh my gosh! Get in the car!"

At dinner, I went around the table, saying the names of the girls until they giggled and rolled their eyes. Sitting in the restaurant where I'd taken Heather on our anniversary, I swelled up when I heard the girl sitting next to Malley turn and whisper, "My dad's never done anything like this."

At The Retro Club near downtown, the sign at the ticket window read "12- to 14-Year-Olds," but judging from the size of the boys who looked like they'd been corn-fed, I was glad that I'd come. Inside, the lighted dance floor vibrated from the songs of the seventies and eighties. A DJ who couldn't have been more than nineteen wore a headset and stood on top of a center platform. He nodded to the beats of songs that I recalled from my days as a boy at the skating rink. Under the floor, colored lights pulsated with the rhythm of the music that blasted from overhead speakers.

The girls took off to the dance floor, worming their way through a flood of kids. Joining the other parents at the edge of the dance floor, I wondered what I would have thought if my own father had escorted me to a place like this at Malley's age. "Waste of money," I could almost hear him say at the very suggestion. Right then while watching my daughter toss her hair and laugh, I was pleased that I'd turned out to be more like my mother. In the past few weeks, I'd told Malley that I loved her more times than I could count. When I was growing up in my dad's household, it seemed that the word *love* was as difficult for him to speak as a foreign language. We were as different as the moon and the sun, and I was determined to pave a completely different trail with my child.

I felt a tug on my hand and turned to see Laci and Emmy, two of Malley's friends, leading me out onto the dance floor. I grooved with the best of them. The words to "Jive Talking" rained down, and suddenly I felt as cocky as the boy in Choctaw who had once skated backwards to impress the group of girls who congregated by the concession stand. I danced and danced and never once thought of spots on X-rays or company organizational charts that no longer included my name.

When she saw me, Malley shook her head and laughed. In the center of a circle of screaming twelve-year-olds, I closed my eyes and, with the beat of the music of my past, shook away the fear of the future. I didn't care if I was embarrassed after the song ended and I faced the stares of the parents; I was living for the moment, and right then the moment felt good.

Malley talked about that night for two days straight, and it took about that long for my legs to stop aching from the dancing. The next day, Malley asked me to take her to get a KC and The Sunshine Band CD, and I gladly complied.

When we returned, I noticed that the car had been backed into the driveway, and the trunk was wide open. Heather came out carrying a suitcase and a pair of shoes. "What's this?" I asked.

"You'll see," Malley said and then jumped from the truck. The trunk of the car was filled with our suitcases and the tote bag full of books usually meant for a beach trip.

"Was this part of some covert operation?"

"You're not the only one with surprises," Heather said. "Malley and I can still manage to pull one over on you."

"What's up with all this?"

"Remember that list?" Malley bit her lower lip. "The list with the chili dogs from that place and that pond and all that stuff?"

"Now, hold on . . ." I struggled to find one common-sense reason why we shouldn't return home for a visit to Choctaw.

"Hold what?" Heather asked. "I've already called Grand Vestal. She's got the place ready for us. She's so excited. She's fixing fried chicken tonight, special for you."

"From the looks of it, you're planning on us staying there until the end of time."

"What does it matter? We have the whole summer," Heather said as she readjusted the suitcases. "It's time, Nathan . . . It's time to run barefoot through that plowed field again."

Chapter Five

Even though her name was Grand Vestal, there was nothing grand about my grandmother except for her heart. She had lived all of her life on a tract of land that my grandfather had managed to farm, if for no other reason, to keep the bill collectors away. Long since widowed, Grand Vestal still lived at the end of the red clay road that was lined with live oaks dating back as far as her people, a small Creek Indian tribe. When the first white man came to the area after the Trail of Tears, the ones who had hidden out in the swamp told them that they were Choctaw Indians, believing that only the Creek Indians were marked for persecution. From then on, the area that eventually grew into a tiny town hovering just above the Florida border was simply called Choctaw.

Grand Vestal greeted us before we could make the bend around the road to her house. Two shirts flapped on a clothesline next to the tin-roofed house with blue shutters shaped like slivers of the moon. She stood on the lowest concrete porch step, its corner chipped away by time. Wiping her hands on a stained yellow rag, she raised it up as if I might have forgotten my way home.

Deep wrinkles lined her eighty-three-year-old face, the skin tanned from hard work and her Indian heritage. She wore the usual polyester navy slacks that belled at the bottom and a sleeveless daisy-print top displaying muscles that women in Atlanta pay trainers to have. The earth was her workout center. She built her arms by continuing to plow her own garden and milk her own cow. Her hair was just as I remembered it. With each step, the gray braids swung from her shoulders with the excitement of a young girl.

She was talking before we could open the car doors. "Eugenia, the woman down at the end of the highway, saw ya'll pull onto my road. She called and said, 'They're turning right now.'"

"How'd she know to look for us?" Malley asked while wrapped in Grand Vestal's arms.

She pulled Malley back and studied her the way she might've if Malley had the measles. "How'd she know . . . how'd she know? Well, you're the brightest thing to land on this side of Georgia since that star fell from the sky and burnt a hole through my barn."

After Grand Vestal hugged Heather, she turned her attention to me. She brushed the hair from my forehead and looked at me so deeply that I had to turn away and point to the dogwood tree that still filled the corner of her yard. "I see that old thing is still around."

"Sugar Boy, that tree's like me. It'll be here till Gabriel blows his trumpet."

That evening we finished off the best fried chicken a man could eat, and I helped Grand Vestal clean the kitchen while Malley and Heather got ready for bed. "You're adrift . . . I see it in the way you move your eyes," she said, running her hands over my forearms. "Your bones are weary too."

Her diagnoses always made me uncomfortable, because nine times out of ten she was right. "I'm fine . . . really. I could plow a garden if you wanted me to."

She straightened the tablecloth and laughed. "You and your garden! You don't know how many times I'm out there working in that pasture and get so tickled. It's a wonder the neighbors don't call the police on me. Sometimes I just howl thinking about . . . you know what I'm fixing to say?"

"The foot thing."

She fanned her hands and giggled. "Yes, gracious, yes. Every time I'm out in that garden, I can just see you running through that dirt barefooted. Your little bird chest just a-heavin' for air."

"Yeah, well, I've still got that bird chest," I said, patting my mending ribs. The very touch caused the spot to cross my mind. It was a distraction that both irritated and reminded me of chores left to be done.

"Did you call and let your daddy know you were coming?" I was hoping she wouldn't ask, but now there was no way out.

"No, I ran out of time."

"Well, now, just so you know . . . he's coming over for dinner tomorrow." I wanted to protest, but there was no use. Facing him and the past would be a task I'd have to handle sooner or later.

I watched her fill a glass of water, which was her nightly routine, and then reach for a plastic lid from a margarine container to keep out the night critters, as she called moths. I felt the pang that comes with being reunited. I could have dictated her moves as good as any Hollywood director. Her habits were stamped in the memories of my childhood and lodged too deep to be stolen.

"Good night, Sugar Boy," she said just before turning out the kitchen light.

Standing in the darkness with the soft rays of moonlight streaming in from the kitchen window, I reached out for her arm and said the words that I should have said all of those times before. "You're something special, Grand Vestal. I haven't said it in a long time . . . but I love you."

Her gasp was quick, and her pat to my arm was even swifter. "You sure do know how to make an old lady proud. I love you too, Sugar Boy. You are a bright spot that lingers around this place." She brushed her thick hand across my face and nodded. "Now, then, we best get to bed because Herman will be a-crowin' soon enough."

"Herman?" I asked, trailing behind her, the hallway boards creaking beneath our weight. "What happened to that other rooster?"

Grand Vestal opened the door to her bedroom. "Oh, you're talking about Augustus. Shoot, he got to crowing too early, so I had to serve him up for Easter dinner."

———

At sunrise Herman went to work. The rooster was loud enough to wake anybody in the vicinity of forty acres. Malley snatched the bedroom door open, her hair tangled and hanging in front of her face. "Can somebody make that bird shut up?" she yelled down the hall.

From the kitchen, Grand Vestal laughed that deep-gutted laugh she had. "Only the good Lord, Miss Mary Sunshine. He's just doing his job, that's all."

It was a strange mix of feelings watching my past and my future meld together. Grand Vestal took Malley out to the barn, and Malley came back forty-five minutes later carrying a bucket of fresh milk and a smile warmer than the plate of biscuits that sat on the table along with grits and sausage. When we finished, Grand Vestal stood and started clearing the table.

"All right, now, I've got a Sunday-morning announcement to make. Anybody who stays under my roof is expected to go to church with me." Heather looked at me wild-eyed, while Malley licked a stream of melting butter from the edge of a biscuit. Church had not exactly been on our weekend schedule back in Atlanta, and the idea of sitting through one of Grand Vestal's church services put a tinge of panic in me.

The pastor I remembered at her church had a black patch over his eye and always brought his pet cockatoo to church. He'd close each service by holding the bird up on his arm and reminding us that if God can take care of the birds of the air, how much more will He do for us? Maybe my doctors back in Atlanta needed to come down here and hear his sermons to remind them that they were not the God who fed the birds or the One who numbered our days.

"Uh . . . let me think if I have something to wear," Heather said as she wiped crumbs from her mouth.

"Shoot! We . . . uh . . . we forgot to bring anything to wear for church." I frowned and shook my head.

"Oh, toot on that. Don't you know the good Lord don't care what you show up in? Just as long as you show up."

Malley looked at my stunned expression and laughed right out loud. She held up her finger and touched the air, making a sizzling sound. "Busted," she whispered.

Opening the refrigerator that was covered in a sea of magnets of every size imaginable, Grand Vestal turned slightly, holding a plate of butter. Her braids flipped across her shoulders. "And don't forget that, after church, your daddy's coming over for dinner."

"So he's coming to church too?" I asked, knowing good and well he was not. Church suited my father the same way a tuxedo did, confining and restrictive.

"No, but he's not sleeping under my roof, now, is he? Now, hurry up and finish so we can get there on time."

———

Before the church service began, the organ swelled with "What a Friend We Have in Jesus" as the Sunday school members filed in through the wooden door next to the altar. Grand Vestal led the way to the same pew she'd occupied since the day the doors opened. She wore a navy dress with a thin belt. The dress had come in and out of fashion through the years, but to my knowledge it had remained the only dress that she owned.

Along the way she stopped by every pew to introduce us. Most of the members of the small red-brick church were people I'd known since I was a boy.

"I think you were just getting married the last time I saw you," Mrs. Harris said, looking Heather up and down. "How long has it been now?"

"Nineteen years," I said and pulled Heather closer to me. "And the honeymoon is still going strong."

Mrs. Harris squealed, and the jiggle of fat under her chin bounced in delight. Grand Vestal shot me a look before turning to the pew across from the aisle.

Homecoming was what the trip to Choctaw Community Church became that day. As the congregation that I'd first known in my younger years stood to sing "When the Roll Is Called Up Yonder," I mouthed the words and listened. Hearing the off-tune, aging voices sing the hymn I knew by heart was sweet medicine, and my soul lapped up every drop.

But not everything had stayed the same in that little

country church that sat next to the highway. The pastor was now a man younger than me. His baritone voice bounced from the plastered walls until not even a child murmured. With each point he wanted to emphasize, he'd run his fingers through his spiky hair and say, "You aren't hearing me, now, are you?"

After the service the pastor greeted us at the door and engulfed Grand Vestal in his arms. She seemed to savor his affection the same way I had savored the hymns about sweet reunions in the sky.

Walking past the cars that lined the gravel parking lot, she lingered to visit with even more people. "Daddy, was Grand Vestal ever mayor of the town or something?" Malley whispered.

"Only in her mind . . . but come to think of it, she'd make a fine one."

When I started to drive away, I asked Grand Vestal what had become of that pastor, the one with an eye patch who brought his cockatoo up to the pulpit.

Fishing through her wicker pocketbook in the backseat of our car, Grand Vestal never looked up. "Oh, him . . . we had to get shut of him, the preacher and that bird both. I tell you, the final straw was Wednesday-night prayer meeting. Racine Taylor was making announcements about visitation, and out of the clear blue, that bird went to screeching and carrying on. You never did hear such a racket. It was just like the very sound of Racine's voice was getting on that bird's nerves. You know, she always did talk through her nose. Well, sir . . . the next thing you know, that bird flew out and plucked Racine's wig right off the top of her head. I mean to tell you, the preacher had a time calming them down . . . Racine and that bird both. They tell me that to this day she still can't walk underneath a tree without getting the nervous shakes."

We laughed and carried on the entire drive back to Grand Vestal's house. I saw my father's truck when we pulled up the long drive, and his outline was visible through the screen porch. His thin frame and slanted shoulders were topped off by the John Deere cap he had worn so long that the logo was only partially readable. "Judging from the looks of it, somebody had a good time," he called out.

"See what you missed, Ronnie Bishop. I declare, the day I get you to church will be the day I'm satisfied the Lord will call me home. My work will finally be done," Grand Vestal said.

"Now, see, that's how come I don't go. I'm working on keeping you around as long as I can help it."

Grand Vestal swatted him on the back with a folded

church bulletin. Malley moved forward and once again became the prim and proper girl from Atlanta whose party manners were paid for in full. My father looked awkward as he first reached for Malley's shoulder and then settled for tussling her hair.

Men might have spoken softer, but I'd never met one who spoke fewer words than my father. The way he'd shift his weight on his feet and fold his arms always made me think that he was never really comfortable in anybody's presence, except my mother's. This homecoming would be no different.

"You're gettin' so big," he said. "Ain't she, Grand Vestal?" My grandmother agreed. "And so pretty. Ain't she pretty, Grand Vestal?" My grandmother agreed again, playing with Malley's hair.

Looking up at him through the screen door framed in cobwebs, his grainy image seemed out of focus. I stood on the concrete step as long as I could, watching him shift his weight as he listened to Malley answer one strained question after another.

Now a man of sixty, he wore gold-rimmed glasses. His ruddy and thick-skinned nose seemed better suited for a man ten years older. A farmer and retired mechanic from the Office of Public Works, he continued to spend more time with his herd of cows than with his own family. He looked through the screen door at me.

"How you making it, Nathan?"

"Good . . . good," I said. "How have you been getting along?"

"Pretty good," he mumbled. "Yep, doing pretty good."

Grand Vestal opened the front door and hung her pocketbook on a coat rack in the foyer. "He's got a hernia on his left side." She never looked back as she offered the report that made my father blush.

"Naw . . . Dr. Lewis didn't say that's for sure."

Grand Vestal yelled over her shoulder, "Don't tell me. Watch how he gives on that left side when he walks. A hernia just as sure as I'm standing here."

Rising up on the toe of his boots, for a second my father seemed taller than me as he tried to examine the porch light. Anything to create a diversion from talking about himself. "Vestal, you heard that Louis Franklin died last night?"

Grand Vestal turned around with her mouth wide open. "What?"

"Garrison told me down at the feed store this morning. He said Louis was just ate up with cancer. Didn't tell a living soul neither, not even his boys."

"Oh, toot," Grand Vestal finally said. "They don't know

what that man had. He caroused every juke joint between here and Albany. I bet a plug nickel that it was his liver that got him."

Somewhere between Louis Franklin's death and Viola Quinton's hip replacement I slipped away from the porch and retreated down the concrete block steps and into the field, where alfalfa grass swayed with the warm spring breeze. The cow Malley and I had moved into the field a day earlier turned and looked at me with pieces of grass still stuck to her lips. Sitting against the fence rail, I heard the screen door squeak and hoped that if I held my breath the person would drift back inside, never spotting the invisible man that glowed with a spot in his chest. But Heather was never one to give up that easy. She opened the rusted fence gate and sat cross-legged next to me. Saying nothing, she simply picked a long blade of grass and twirled it around her finger.

"What are you doing out here?" she said finally, slapping my arm with the blade of grass.

Shrugging, I fought the urge to say nothing and to make her go back inside. But as foolish as I might have been, I knew that she was the one sure thing that I couldn't afford to push away. So instead, I put my arm around her and buried my nose in her lilac-scented hair.

"Don't think you're going to get me to change the subject by doing that."

"What?" I whispered.

"You know what. Listen, why can't you be this nice in front of your daddy?"

"I've studied that one for years. The best I can come up with is that he's the moon and I'm the sun. Go figure."

"All right." Heather nodded in agreement. "But you know what they say about the moon: it has no reflection without the sun."

Her words poured into my being, and I was left staring at the cows that had moved closer to the edge of a dried pond, their steps making crackling sounds in the caked mud.

"To be honest with you, he just rubs me the wrong way."

Heather's touch was soft to my arm. "I want so badly for this visit to be harmonious. Can't you look for the common good in your daddy instead of trying to change him? It's there, you know. You just have to dig for it." She kissed me on the cheek and walked back to the house, but her words stayed on my mind. I tried to think of the common good that Heather claimed stretched between my father and me. Even his features were not mine. I was my mother's son and had her dark hair and green eyes to prove it. My father's hair was redder, auburn in color like the hair that Malley was born with. The one thing that my mind kept going back to was the fact that my mother loved him for forty-two years. Time and again after my mother died, Grand Vestal would remind me that my father was a good man, as if saying it often enough would convince me.

"What makes you say that . . . that you know he's good?" I'd always ask.

"Because my daughter loved him till the day she died."

I'm sure Grand Vestal was right. When I was a boy Mama would sit on my father's lap and snuggle on his chest as we watched TV. I'd see her primp in the mirror before he was due home from work and then run to kiss him when he walked through the door. But what about his love for her? If there was so much love, then why did he leave her alone on the night she died?

Venturing back to the house for the sake of keeping peace with my wife, if for no other reason, I found my father sitting on the porch step, still trying to make conversation.

"Daddy, did you tell Grandpa Ron where we're going?" Malley asked.

"Where might that be?" my father asked.

"Uh . . . I thought I'd take her down to Brouser's Pond. Do a little bass fishing."

"He made this list of places he wanted to visit," Malley said. "I'm gonna make sure we hit every one of them."

"What all's on this list?" my father asked.

"Some place that sells chili dogs," Malley said.

"Suit yourself, but I'd rather catch me a bass than wind up with a case of indigestion from Holster's Drive-In," my father said.

Malley laughed and, on cue, my father laughed right along with her.

"Hey," I said. I paused, not sure if I really wanted to say what I was thinking. My father and Malley looked up at me and waited. "Um . . . why don't you come out to Brouser's with us? You still know the best places, don't you?"

"I reckon we can do that." My father pushed up the brim of his cap and leaned forward. "'Bout what time you want me to come by in the morning?"

After setting a time after breakfast, I opened the door to walk into the house but paused at the step and patted his shoulder. The roughness of the plaid shirt seemed appropriate for this man who had never to my knowledge spoken the word *love*.

He looked up at me with that squinted look and smiled wide enough to reveal a missing tooth in the far corner of his mouth.

If only for an afternoon, the weight of tension that had held my father and me down so tight that I thought at times I'd bust had been lifted. Just like I knew she would, Malley took our relationship up in a hot-air balloon called hope.

Chapter Six

Dew still covered the ground, and the sun had not yet completely risen over the treetops when my father's red pickup appeared. Grand Vestal was stuffing Malley's book bag with biscuits and a Mason jar filled with green tea. "This tea will give you strength to reel in a big one," Grand Vestal said before sending her off with a kiss. "Now, Sugar Boy, you sip on that tea too. It'll do you good."

Riding through downtown for the first time, I felt a sense of sadness drift over me as we passed vacant buildings that had thrived with business during my youth. Only the newspaper office and the Johnston family hardware store had remained intact. "Nothing stays the same," I mumbled.

Brouser's Pond was appropriately located behind Gil Brouser's house. Fifty years ago his father had bought the property that circled the pond. Even though it was private property, anybody in Choctaw was welcome to fish as long as they left a dollar in an old coffee can that dangled from a rusted nail on a pine tree. Gil's dog chased the dust behind us just like we chased the low clouds that hung over the pond. Vines and tree limbs scratched at the truck, but my father never paid them any mind. He stared straight ahead, his eyes fixated on the body of water that awaited us. Water remained the one place where his eyes would widen and his words would broaden into short conversations.

At the pond, we found a spot along the bank above a patch of lily pads covered in white flowers. "Let me fix your line for you," I said to Malley, but when I turned, my father had already taken a pair of pliers to her spinning reel. He stood frozen, looking at me, and offered up the line for me to fix. Shaking my head, I said, "It looks like you've got it all worked out."

"Careful not to get too close to those weeds on the bank. You don't want to surprise a moccasin." My words never impacted headstrong Malley. She adjusted her sunglasses and pulled down the John Deere cap that she'd taken from the gun rack in my father's truck. Grinning, I could only imagine what her big-city friends would say about this girl who'd gone country.

A crow called out as it landed on a pine tree limb above us. My father never looked away from the pond as he reeled in his line. As a boy, I loved to watch his arm muscles flinch and jerk with the movement of the fishing pole.

The reflection of the water against his sunglasses and the way he seemed hypnotized had caused me to imagine that he'd grown up in the pond. I created a story worthy of a comic superhero and even secretly named him Bassman.

Now ripples of water floated across the pond and the humming of our spinning reels called out. "What's all this business about your lung?" He cast his line but never looked at me.

My neck tightened with the question. Heather or Malley had obviously told him. At first I pretended that I hadn't heard his question. I wanted the high-pitched whine of the reels to block out the reality of the present.

"Yeah, that . . . you know, I had this accident at work, and while I was in the hospital, the doctors found this thing . . . this spot. But nobody knows for sure. I mean, they said I could've been born with it."

My father jerked the line of his fishing rod and then mumbled. "You okay with everything?"

His question struck me sideways, hooking me in to the truth.

"Well, not much I can do about it. I have to be okay with it. I mean, I don't want to get sicker taking treatment like . . . like some people."

Adjusting the anchors on his line, my father stopped

and let the hook dangle. His eyes were not glassy like the pond; they were slate blue and focused only on me. "The way I figure it, everybody's terminal. Some just at different stages than others."

Stepping closer, I wanted to hear his words again and to hang on to the reassurance of his voice, but Malley's scream cut through me deeper than his wisdom. She was pulling with all of her might and fighting a rod that was bending lower to the water. "Don't let go," I yelled.

She slid down lower into the grassy bank. Gripping her rod, I thought the pole was going to snap in two— along with my ribs. Just when I thought the pain in my chest was going to cause me to let my daughter down, the rough hands of my father were on top of mine. He was behind me, pulling and grunting all at the same time.

"I'm going overboard," Malley kept screaming as we slid lower to the water's edge. Oil-colored water sloshed over her pink tennis shoes.

"Just keep a-pulling," my father yelled. And pull we did. We pulled until I felt every muscle in my back tighten. It felt good to finally fight for something worthwhile.

"Give it a big yank on three," my father said. "One, two, three . . . ." With that final jerk we all landed flat on our tails, and the biggest bass I'd ever laid eyes on flapped at the water's edge. Jumping at him, I fell face-first into the water and threw that fish as far to the bank as I could. Malley and my father struggled to pull him up the rest of the way. I laughed out loud looking at Malley. The John Deere cap was knocked sideways, and her designer sunglasses dangled from her nose, making her look like an old lady. "Go, Malley! Go, Malley!" I yelled, churning the water with my hands. I jumped up and down on the muddy floor of that pond and hollered loud enough for all of Choctaw to hear me. It felt good to cheer for my baby girl.

Back at Grand Vestal's, Heather took a picture of the three of us with Malley pointing to the fifteen-pound bass hanging from the fence post. I hung the photo on the refrigerator door as a reminder to jump in with both feet and savor the victories.

After supper Malley was still basking in her triumph when she emerged into the living room carrying an oak box decorated with carved doves.

"Whatcha got there?" I asked, sipping the latest herb tea that Grand Vestal had placed before me.

"I don't know, but it was underneath my bed, covered in bubble paper." Malley sat the box down in the middle of the floor and started to unlatch the gold lock.

Heather leaned forward from the easy chair where she sat curled up, reading a book. "Hold it. This is Grand Vestal's house. So, therefore, that makes it her box. Don't you think you should ask permission before you start plundering around?"

Grand Vestal walked from the kitchen carrying a dish towel. She looked down at the box and into the wide green eyes of Malley, who was kneeling next to it.

"I found this under the bed. Can I look through it?"

Grand Vestal sat on the edge of the sofa and ran the tip of her finger over the gold handle. "I expect you should. It's gonna be yours someday."

Malley looked at me, and I only shrugged.

"It was my daughter's hope chest. Your grandmama's. Her dreams are tucked away in there. One day I expect you'll put your hopes in there too."

Getting on the floor next to Malley, I found myself running my hand over the carved grooves. "I never saw this."

"You'd be surprised," Grand Vestal said and winked. "You might recognize a thing or two in it." Grand Vestal opened up the box, and the smell of aged cedar flowed through the living room.

My father came out of the kitchen and joined us in the living room as we pulled out the clippings from the paper about my mother, Barbara Rickers, playing in a piano recital. Grand Vestal sat on the sofa, touching each item as it was passed to her. Malley pulled out an old black-and-white photograph of my mother and father with their arms wrapped around each other and handed it to my father. "Now, who is this ugly, skinny boy standing next to that pretty gal?" he asked. Army barracks and snow were scattered in the background of the photo. Even though she had a coat on and her hands were tucked in the coat pockets, you could still tell that my mama was pregnant.

Grand Vestal leaned over the sofa so she could see the photograph. "That was in Colorado when Ronnie was serving in the army." She swatted his arm. "Umm, it liked to have tore me to pieces the day you took my girl so far away."

My father shifted his weight in the chair and reached over to examine a figurine of a dog on the table next to him.

"That's where I was born," I said.

Malley looked deeper into the picture as if she might be able to see through the coat and my mother's womb and find me.

While we all laughed at the styles from the past and listened to Grand Vestal tell stories about the pictures, I dug out a gold-colored photo album with drawings of trees etched across the cover. The album and the smell of its pages teased the farthest corners of my mind.

When I opened the album and saw the yellowed newspaper clippings, it hit me. Suddenly, I was once again with my mother, sitting at our kitchen table in the green-vinyl chairs and talking about the distant places she would clip from the Sunday travel section of the Valdosta newspaper. Smelling the pages, I hoped that the strawberry scent of her perfume was still locked inside.

"What are you smelling?" Malley asked.

"The past," I said, never taking my nose from the pages. I started to flip through the book of my mother's dreams. Articles on the Empire State Building, Miami Beach, and the Oregon coastline stretched before me. "These are all the places that I want to see," my mother would say as she clipped the newspaper pages. "When we going, Mama?" I'd ask. "One day," she'd say, never taking her eyes from the exotic pictures that teased us. "Maybe one day."

But one day never arrived in time for my mama. A tumor on her pancreas had caused a detour, and by then the journey was too far off in the horizon. Flipping through the pages that were dedicated to the Grand Canyon, the weight of regret felt as heavy as the clay-colored mountains in the photograph. That was the trip that came the closest to becoming reality. Mama had already made the reservations at a campground that she promised would be just as exciting as the one the Brady Bunch had visited on TV. But a new tractor took precedent over an extravagant trip. "We got to use common sense around here," my father had said the night he came home with the tractor. "Besides, that big old hole in the ground will still be there later on," he added as he flicked a toothpick in the corner of his mouth. My mama only winked and forced a smile as I folded my arms and leaned back against the vinyl chair. "Maybe one day," she whispered while reaching for my plate. "Maybe one day."

"What do you remember most about Grandmama?" Heather asked, smiling at Malley. Emotion hung in the back of my throat, and for a moment I feared that it might choke me. A sentimental journey with my father was not what I was wanting. Not as I was holding the book of my mother's lost dreams.

"Cornbread," Malley said and laughed. She brushed the hair from her eyes and said, "It was sweet like cake or something."

"What about you, Grand Vestal? What do you miss?" Heather searched Grand Vestal and then looked at me. How could Grand Vestal offer up only one thing that she missed about her firstborn child?

"Sweet smiles." Grand Vestal said. "That little smile of hers warmed my heart the first time she let me see it. The day I was sitting over yonder, nursing her. Then that smile warmed my heart all over again the last time I saw her, the day she drifted away. The Lord's been good to me."

The sounds of chirping birds rolled into the house, but no one else stirred. We just sat there staring at a scrapbook that they all saw as sweet reminders. I saw the book of clippings only as lost opportunities. Malley looked over at the scrapbook in my hands.

"What's that a picture of, Daddy?"

I snapped the book closed.

Rising, my father coughed before standing to his feet. The conversation was too much for him; he didn't want to talk about my mother any more than I did.

"It's a picture of the Grand Canyon," I said before he could make it past the hall table that held the phone and the figurines.

My father stopped, and for the first time I saw the back of his neck. It was lined with wrinkles as deep as those of an old man. His jeans dropped lower, and part of his denim shirt hung free from the waist of his pants.

"There was this trip we planned one time. Back when I was a little boy. Mama sat up late planning that trip to the

Grand Canyon for days on end. She even had me to draw the colors that I thought we'd find spread out across that big open space."

"Were they the colors you thought they'd be?" Malley asked.

Shrugging, I flicked the corner of my mouth with my tongue. It was a feat to hold my words back, but the trick failed. "I can't tell you, because we never made that trip. Maybe one day. Right, Daddy? Maybe one day."

Never turning to face us, my father nodded and then made his way out of the house. The sound of his boots hitting the wooden floor echoed even after he'd made it through the doorway.

I walked into the kitchen and watched him get into his truck. The floodlight from the back porch spread out across the truck like he was an actor in a play.

Grand Vestal snuck up beside me and snaked her arm around me. She leaned so close that I could make out the mushroom-shaped age spots that dotted her hairline.

"You know something? As many years as I've known your daddy, I still don't know him. But there's one thing I'm satisfied of: Ronnie Bishop is a good man. His heart is good."

"I keep on wanting to believe that."

"Then keep on trying," she said. "Throw off that anger that's pinning you down. Let yourself be free."

She walked away and then stopped when she got to the shelf lined with family photos of our past and future. "You're at a crossroads. And Sugar Boy, you're the only one who can decide which way to go. Not me, not your wife, and not that daddy of yours. Listen to this old lady, because she knows what she's talking about. Time's a gift handed down to each one of us. Don't waste that gift by wrestling things you can't change."

After everyone went to bed, I sat at the kitchen table, flipping through the pages of the scrapbook my mother had put together. Something in the deepest part of me broke free that night, and with it came a flood of resentment that I'd long since locked away. The kitchen light cast a shadow over the clippings now yellowed and stained with age. Then, in the quiet of the night, with those I loved already tucked in bed, I pressed my head against the kitchen table and cried. The paper that had first been touched by my mother and held her dreams now carried the tears of my regrets, the tears of my past.

Chapter Seven

By the second week in Choctaw, Heather was spending her days making contact with old friends from high school. The Walker twins, who ran the only dress store and travel agency in town, were regular lunchtime partners. They'd congregate at the deli that had set up business next to their shop at the old train depot. Lana, the sister with the biggest teeth, usually came by the house in a convertible Volkswagen Bug to pick Heather up. Swaying back and forth as she hugged Heather, Lana looked over Heather's shoulder and saw me standing on the porch step with my hands tucked in my pockets. "Nathan Bishop . . . I swear, how long has it been?" Lana squealed as she came prancing toward me like she might still be homecoming queen, a long, sheer jacket flowing behind her.

I patted my chest, "Still mending."

"You look good," she said, talking loud and patting my arm. All the while she stared at my chest as if trying to figure out the exact location where the spot lived. "I mean, to have cheated death and everything." She and Heather quickly got into the car. "Come on and go with us," she said.

"Naw, there's enough for me to do around here."

Lana grinned to reveal those shiny teeth that I remembered. "Now, before the summer's over, we're going to have a big cookout," she yelled while buckling her seat belt. "A high-school reunion of sorts. It'll be just like old times again."

Watching them drive away, I felt myself becoming more a part of the ten acres that surrounded Grand Vestal's place. I imagined being in exile, unable to step foot past the fence post at the edge of the road, exiled from the townspeople who I'm sure had already started thinking about the type of flowers they might send to my funeral. It was the part of small-town life that I didn't miss, so I chose not to worry with them unless they happened to drive into the kingdom known as Grand Vestal's.

My father was the only regular visitor each day. He showed up every afternoon right after his nap and always stayed exactly one hour. He sat at the kitchen table, listening to Grand Vestal's updates about our morning activities. I wondered why he never asked me why I didn't drop by to see him. But I guess the memories of the past were still too fresh for both of us, and the inner wounds were not yet healed. He was there the day the Walker sisters took Heather to lunch.

Before I could close the front door, Grand Vestal was talking. "Was that Henry Walker's daughter that Heather went out to eat with?"

"Yes, ma'am."

Grand Vestal folded the newspaper that she was reading. "She has a twin too, right? The one that runs the dress shop."

"Yes, ma'am. But they just opened up a travel agency too."

My father was leaning over the table, rolling the salt shaker between his fingers. "I've been studying about taking a vacation."

"Vacation?" Grand Vestal cried. "You're thinking of taking a vacation?" My father nodded. "Where on earth to?"

"Don't know yet. Thinking about seeing some of the country."

Grand Vestal fanned herself with the newspaper. "Ronnie Bishop, has the heat got the best of you? You haven't ventured past the county line since Moses was a boy." With the exception of his stint in the service, my father had never left Georgia.

"Just been thinking that it's time for me to see the country while I still got my health."

"When are you going?" Malley asked as she passed through to the kitchen.

"Don't know yet."

"Is anybody going with you on this vacation of yours?" Grand Vestal asked.

When my father shrugged off the question, Grand Vestal threw down the newspaper. "Lord have mercy! I could get more information from the fence post out there." She got up and started dusting the coffee table. Recreation and day-dreaming were now officially over. There was work to be done.

After my father left, I tossed a bale of hay over the fence into the pasture. As the cows trotted toward the fence, I brushed away pieces of hay that clung to my shirt, and that's when it hit me. For the first time I had taken on a physical job without my ribs causing me to grimace. The cows looked up when I cheered; the yell made me feel twice as good about being free from the pain.

———

By Memorial Day, the summer heat landed on Grand Vestal's house with a seduction of laziness that she never tolerated. While a portable fan rotated on the back porch next to a pile of watermelons, we weeded out the garden and fought the streams of sweat that stung our eyes. Malley pushed her bandanna back higher on her head but never complained. "Sweat is nothing but a sign of honest work," Grand Vestal said. The definition might as well have been scratched across the sand of her garden. I wondered if there was some sort of magic in the way that she had said the words that kept a twelve-year-old girl from griping.

"This row is mine," Malley pulled back stalks of corn and yelled.

"Yours?" I asked, pulling weeds from around the tomato plants.

"It's hers, all right." Grand Vestal said from one row over. "She's going to work two rows all by herself. Then when we take the produce to market in Valdosta, she'll pocket the money too."

The sun burned against our skin the same way that it cooked the soil. Grains of sand fell from our fingertips like pieces of grilled peppercorn. Then the sound of crackling gravel and tires hitting the washed-out place in Grand Vestal's driveway caused us all to walk out from the garden like actors stepping from behind a green curtain.

Coming around the side of the house was my father's red pickup, pulling a white travel trailer with a red stripe down the side. Swinging around the clothesline, my father pulled up to the edge of the porch and stepped out, grinning as big as he had the day Malley caught the bass.

"Ronnie Bishop, what've you gone and done now?"

My father reached up and tapped the side of the camper. "They auctioned off Louis Franklin's belongings at the feed store this morning. His boy claims this trailer hasn't yet seen five hundred miles. Louis never got out much."

"You went and bought a fifth-wheel camper?" Grand Vestal pulled her neck close to her chest until it looked like she might have a roll of fat. "What business do you have spending money on such as that?"

Shrugging, my father kicked at a stone in the dirt. "I told you I wanted to take a look at the country."

"In that thing?" Grand Vestal asked with her hands propped against her waist.

"A man gets tired of looking at four walls all the time."

"Where on earth are you planning to go? A man your age has got no business traveling by himself neither. Next thing you know, somebody will have knocked you in the head and taken off with that camper and your wallet both."

Malley ran up to the trailer and opened the door. She was still standing there, peering inside, when my father said the words that made them all stare at me.

"If somebody was wanting to . . . oh, I don't know . . . go out west . . . maybe to that big hole out in Arizona . . . you reckon any of ya'll might go with me?"

Grand Vestal and Malley stepped slowly toward me the same way they might act if they were trying to catch a feral cat that had darted away at the first sign of affection. Their wide-eyed stares burned holes through the excuses that raced through my mind.

———

That night, sitting on the edge of the bed beside Heather, I said, "I can't do it."

"You can't, or you won't?" she asked. I rubbed my head while the details swirled around me.

"Fine. You know what? I don't want to go."

"Why not? Like you told Malley the night you took her and her friends dancing, 'What if this trip goes down as one of the best times of your life?'"

"That's a low blow, using a man's own words against him."

Heather laughed and leaned into me. "Seriously, Nathan, you'll regret it if you don't go. Trust me. You'll regret the what-if, and if I recall, you recently told me that you didn't want to live your life by 'what if.'"

I threw up my hands. "There you go again, using my words against me! Why did I have to hook up with a woman with the memory of an elephant?" She laughed again and then left me alone to sort out a decision.

Walking around the bedroom, I fought the nervousness of finally coming face-to-face with my father on a trip that would take days on end, sitting in a pickup, staring at the empty asphalt before us. What would we talk about? How would we ever get beyond the silence? I kept thinking it was a mistake, but the part of me that had decided to live saw only the adventure that lay ahead. My smart-aleck comments to my father were now swinging me by the tail. It was time to either take action like a man or to quit whining like a baby.

I slipped out to the back porch and flipped through the places that my mother had once dreamed of visiting. Until Malley had found the scrapbook, her dreams had been buried right along with her. For me the scrapbook became a textbook of lessons learned from putting off for tomorrow what should be carried out today. Not taking the trip that she had longed for would be the same as letting her down. Rubbing the top of the photo album that held my mother's dreams, I knew that the trip was meant for her as much as it was for me. A journey for those who had wanted to live.

—

The next morning Grand Vestal filled jugs of water in the kitchen and handed them to me. "You need to drink well water with some nutrients in it." She moved about the kitchen gathering ginseng, green teas, and other spinach-looking juices that she claimed ate up toxins.

Before I walked outside, I searched the living room, trying to sear the details in my mind. The smell of ash and smoke from the wood-burning stove and the way Grand Vestal's glasses were laid across the Bible on the scratched-up coffee table. Pausing at the door, I fought the feeling that I might never pass this way again.

By the time I'd loaded the luggage, Grand Vestal had finished organizing the small kitchen in the camper and securing the boxes that she'd prepared for us. Sweat trickled from her brow as she pushed back the lose ends of hair. "Bye, Sugar Boy." She patted me three times the way she always did for luck. "Just keep your eyes on the path ahead of you. Don't look to the right or to the left. Then you'll find what you need."

"Yes ma'am. Take care of my girls for me," I said, winking at Heather and Malley. Heather wrapped her arms around my neck. "Can I talk you into going with us?" I asked, whispering in her ear.

"No," she said, kissing me. "It's time, Nathan. Time to do this on your own." I leaned over and hugged Malley. She handed me my mother's scrapbook.

"Here, don't forget this." She smiled when I squeezed her extra hard.

"You're still my baby girl," I whispered in her ear.

My father sat in his truck, sipping from a white thermos stained with coffee. He seemed startled when I walked up next to the truck window, like he was unsure whether I'd really make the trip. He wiped the spilled coffee from the pocket of his shirt and nodded at me.

The truck door creaked as I closed it, and the sweetness of cow feed that my father transported from the feed store every Friday engulfed me. It was the same scent that I'd smelled in the truck the day he taught me how to drive in the pasture.

My father never said a word as we left Choctaw, Georgia, that summer day. He just honked the horn and tossed a hand out the window and saluted. Malley and Heather stood on the same concrete step where Grand Vestal had first greeted us. I kept watch over them long after they had slipped away from my view.

———

Up until we'd reached Alabama, my father had been satisfied to eat sausage and crackers from one of the supply boxes that Grand Vestal had packed for us. By the time we were north of Birmingham, though, he was ready to stop at a diner and have a real meal.

Inside, the Shiny Diner lived up to its name with chrome booths fastened with red vinyl cushions. A young woman with a ponytail took our order. When she served the plates of meat loaf, she paused before turning to walk away. "You have got to be father and son."

Chewing a piece of bread, I looked up at the same time my father did. "Yeah," we both said and she walked away, nodding.

When she brought the check to the table, I asked her how she knew we were father and son. With her head tossed back, she said, "This is just a part-time thing. I'm working on a psychology paper and use this job to help pick out father-son connections. I'm calling it 'Male Connections.'"

"You don't say," I said and reached for a toothpick from the jukebox-shaped container at the end of the table.

"It's always the same. They order the same foods, give the same looks to each other, but yet . . . there's seldom any talking. Just mainly looks."

She ripped the ticket from the pad, and I snatched the check before my father could grab it. "It's on me this time."

"I'll pick up the tip, then." My father pulled himself out of the booth by gripping the chrome tabletop. He never acknowledged the waitress or her observations that jolted me to the core of my insides. Make no mistake about it, I had not left my family behind to spend time communicating to my father through our mutual love of meat loaf. I was going to know him right down to the DNA that we shared but never discussed. It would be a journey that tested the limits of my patience more than any project deadline I'd ever faced at Beckett Construction.

Chapter Eight

Driving down the middle of America on Interstate 40, hotel chains and fast-food restaurants filled the open spaces just as country music and talk radio filled the gaps of silence inside the truck. With each state line we passed, I found myself missing Heather and Malley more and more, until I almost gave in and asked Dad to turn around. The old part of me that kept wanting to resurrect my obsession with time told me that this was all a waste, a trip better suited for an airplane, with my wife and daughter, people who actually liked to talk. The steady tread of the truck tires caused the passenger door to vibrate against my shoulder, and I gave in and leaned closer until my face was pressed against the side of the window. Pretending to sleep, I kept a vigil over the green clock on the truck dashboard. An hour later we pulled over at a rest stop.

Outside of Oklahoma City, a billboard advertising the Championship Rodeo greeted us with an outline of a cowboy holding his hat in one hand and gripping the rope on a bucking bull with the other. Nodding at the sign, my father said, "They played a rodeo taped there on TV the other night." He chuckled and gripped the steering wheel tighter. "I wondered if we'd pass that place."

"Let's stop."

He glanced at me and quickly looked back at the inter-state. "Naw. We best not."

"Why not?"

He ran his hands over the steering wheel before finally settling for driving with one hand on top of the wheel and one on the bottom. "We got that canyon to see."

"Well, if it's been there this long, I bet it will still be there whenever we make it. Come on, live a little."

The words seemed to startle him right down to the toes of his boots. He grimaced and then coughed.

Why am I even wasting my breath? I leaned back against the passenger window. The tops of houses and downtown streets flashed below. The bullheadedness of Ron Bishop was a surprise at every turn, and all of a sudden I was staring at the tall Greyhound bus station sign off in the distance.

The ticking of the blinker rang out against the soft country music that played on the truck radio. Rising up, I noticed that we were going down a bypass ramp. "I think you keep on going straight, don't you?"

"Not if you want to see the rodeo, you don't."

———

The fancy pavilion called Longhorn Center was not exactly what I'd call roughing it. The red and beige building housed lights and catwalks good enough for any Las Vegas show. Standing at the ticket booth, talking to a woman who wore a black cowboy shirt with silver arrows stitched across the chest, it was no surprise to learn that Elvis had even been in the building at one time.

"Who's the meanest, baddest bull out there?" I asked the cashier through the vents in the glassed window.

The heavy woman flipped through my change and gave me a frightful look. Her coworker, a girl wearing silver bangles and occupying the adjacent stool, wasted no time in hitting a button on the panel next to the register. Just when I expected security to show up and book me for being overly nice, the girl smiled and her soft voice drifted from the speaker. "FuManChu."

"Him, huh?"

Shaking her head, the girl's dark eyes grew wider. "Oh yeah. You'll see."

Inside the arena my father came to life as the smell of popcorn and spilled beer overpowered the scent of livestock.

We watched from the middle row as man after man got his tail worn out by the bucking bulls that made the riders seem like nothing more than rag dolls. Eight seconds was all that they were after, but I'm sure that to the riders it seemed like eternity.

The announcer who sounded fresh from a radio station told us that Tony Camber from Lubbock would be riding FuManChu. A hiss sounded from the audience, and one man stood up and put his cap over his heart. The gray-and-white bull flew out of the chute, kicking wildly. From the start his head spun like he was having a seizure, a seizure meant to shock the man from Lubbock right into the dirt. The rider bounced back and forth on the bull just like a windup toy. Yelling some shrill sound of fury, the cowboy kept a smile on his face. He was kicking the tar out of this bull, and no matter how rough it got, the man was not going to let go until he was bucked completely off and flat on his back. Edging closer to the end of my seat, I could almost feel the rider's adrenaline as he lived a life that his mama refused to want to know about.

In no time, the bull won, or so he thought. Before he ran away, the cowboy reached for his hat from the ground, bowed, and then ran from the arena, laughing loud enough for us to hear it up in the bleachers.

A clown circled a red-and-white barrel, waving a handkerchief to coax the bull through a side gate. The bull kicked at the dirt, anger packed in the muscles of his shanks. He snorted with fire, and a cloud of dust whirled over his back.

The dance went back and forth between the bull and clown while the audience jumped to their feet, gasping and yelling with each turn of the bull. Able to make a jump for it, the clown landed in the barrel and was pushed twenty yards. A hush fell over the pavilion, and we all leaned forward. Looking up to the grandstands, the bull seemed to be staring right at me as he snorted and kicked the dirt. Never looking away, I watched while he shook his head in a rage that I don't think man has ever known.

The bull's attention soon drifted back to the barrel, and after giving it one more push with his head, he turned and slowly walked back to the gate with the audience hissing every step of his stride.

My father licked back the spit of his excitement and nudged me. "That one liked to tore him up. That fella can sure say he did something tonight, riding that bull the way he did."

I'd never seen my father that full of life before. He sat on the edge of his seat, hands propped on his knees, waiting and watching for the next movement in the arena. His enthusiasm was that of a boy at the circus, watching a man walk a tightrope while balancing a pole of fire.

Later, when he got hungry again, my father slipped out to the truck for a piece of sausage and a smoke break. He didn't say it, but I knew he didn't want me inhaling the cigarette smoke, most likely out of fear that it would feed my white spot.

After the barrel-racing event, I made my way back through the halls lined with photos of the famous that had visited the arena. A sign read "Staff Only," but I kept going. Sometimes when you're living like there's no tomorrow, you just have to learn to ignore signs meant to hold you back.

Through a set of double doors, I found the place I'd been expecting all along. Bulls were packed into stalls until some showed their anger by racking the iron gates with their horns. The smell of sweat and manure overpowered that of the popcorn that flowed from inside the air-conditioned arena. Walking past a group of men with their feet propped on a feed bucket, I nodded and kept going. The bull that fought harder than the rest was what I'd come to find, and somewhere within the iron gates, he was waiting, snorting and stomping in a rage that nobody else could possibly understand.

A woman with a T-shirt and short gray hair was holding a hose and filling up a bucket of water hanging inside one of the stalls. She laughed at the man standing next to her and then glanced in my direction. A man with a handlebar mustache and coal-colored eyes kicked his boot against the gate and laughed harder than the woman. "I'm not lying to you. That's just the way it happened." His words trailed off, but his smile never wavered. "Afternoon," he called out.

"Afternoon. Looks like ya'll are keeping busy," I said.

"Always, my friend. Always."

The woman murmured "Excuse me," and pulled the water hose to the next stall.

"Sure are a lot of bulls," I said and then feared the stupid remark would cause me to get thrown out before I'd come face-to-face with the one thing that was madder than me.

The man laughed in a graveled, smoker sort of way and then spat tobacco on the asphalt, inches from my feet. "You looking for a bull in particular?"

I scanned the livestock pavilion like I was searching for a lost friend. "That gray one . . . that one named something-Chew."

"FuManChu," the man said nodding. His smile grew wider with each syllable, and he motioned for me to fol-low him. "That bull paid off my truck and a second wife."

"What, you mean you own him?" I asked, trying not to follow too far behind him and make him think I was some boy.

When he turned slightly, his hooked nose stuck out like a claw. "I bought that bull six years ago. Nothing but a scrawny railroad rat. You could count his ribs. The man down in Belmont who sold him to me told me I was the first natural-born fool he'd ever met. But there was this thing about that bull's eyes." The man stopped and pointed to his own eye. "He liked to have stared a hole through me. He held up that head just as straight as you please like he thought he was somebody . . . and him half dead. Right then I knew that bull still had vinegar left in him."

At the corner gate next to the livestock trailers that lined the parking lot, I saw the look, up close and personal. The bull snorted and trotted around the small stall like he was insulted not to have more room. His horns raked down the side of the iron rails, and I fought from jumping back. Noticing my hesitation anyway, the man laughed. "He'll flat sure put a hurting on you."

Staring into the slanted eyes of the bull, eyes that seemed better suited for an alligator, I kept the gaze until the bull turned and circled the other side of the stall.

Looking at that bad boy, I felt every ounce of adventure that I'd pushed back over the years flood to the surface. The words spewed out as fast as the beat of my heart. "How much will you take to let me ride him?"

In the snack bar with a buffalo head hanging over us, we negotiated the details while rodeo fans drifted by, filling their cups with ice and soft drinks from a dispenser.

Ham, I learned the man was called, sat back in the chair and tipped the hat from his brow. "Man, you mean to tell me you never rode a bull and you're wanting to start with mine? Huh-uh," Ham said shaking his head. "It can't be done."

"Says who? Look, I'll take lessons, clean the stalls, pitch a tent in your backyard . . . whatever it is you think I need to do to get me on that bull."

Ham laughed and picked up a straw from the drink-stained table. With a piece of the straw in his mouth, his dark eyes focused on me. "Now, let's get to it. What's really behind this?"

Watching a woman wearing a denim shirt with a rose stitched on the back move toward the drink machine, I tried to organize my words with caution, knowing that if he didn't see it my way, I'd be back on the road with my father, and FuManChu would be back home in his pen.

"The thing is, all my life I've played it safe, never taking real chances. Then something happened . . . I found out I had a spot on my lung and the job I thought only I could do got turned over to somebody else. My world got knocked upside down. You know, looking at the world from a different angle, you figure some things out pretty fast. Somewhere back there I stopped living and ended up a walking dead man. I'm fighting to make sure that never happens again."

Chewing the straw, Ham kept a gaze on me the same as I had on his bull. A voice called out over the intercom that the pole-bending event was about to start, and I got up to leave. I'd had my say. Now it was time to move on.

Before I could get past the drink machine, Ham's graveled voice called out. "You gonna have to sign a release. You got a problem with that?"

Turning, I smiled and said, "Don't worry. That's one thing I'm getting pretty good at."

After Ham came to terms on a fair price for training me, my father and I drove out to his place north of town. He lived on a state road dotted with farmhouses and scrub oaks. His place had a painted sign that looked like homemade: Rancho FuManChu. Seeing as how the bull was his prized possession, I wasn't as surprised by the name as my father. "Naming someplace after a bull," he mumbled and pulled into the driveway littered with crushed beer cans and rocks.

I'd figured that my father would've been harder to convince than Ham, but after vowing that he wouldn't call Heather, he rubbed his chin and shook his head. "We're all terminal, remember," I said.

A black-and-brown sheep dog met us at the house. His tongue was dripping from the dry heat. "Shadow, get back here," Ham yelled as he eased down the back deck that hung from his house. South Fork Ranch, it wasn't. Ham's modest block home with dusty red shutters looked more like a garage with some windows tacked on to the front. Rows of birdhouses painted in different colors of the rainbow were scattered across the deck railing. "You made these?" I asked.

"Yeah, gives me something to do between gigs with FuManChu. Sell 'em at the rodeos."

"How much does a house like that one with the church steeple go for?"

"Depends," Ham said, rubbing his jaw and looking back at the birdhouse. "Between seventy-five and a hundred."

Ham flipped on a light switch inside the tin-roof building that housed a lawnmower and a mismatched set of two-by-fours. The smell of planting manure and gaso-line met us at the door. Ham never seemed to notice when he kicked over a bucket and nails scattered across the concrete floor.

"Now, this here is what they call the electric bull," Ham said while yanking a blue, tattered blanket from the machine. Underneath, a saddle-shaped iron machine was bowed down in submission. "You ever seen one of these before?"

I stopped short of commenting about the one I'd seen in the movie *Urban Cowboy* and just shook my head no.

After Ham jumped up on the machine backwards and held up his fingers to show me how to grip the rope, I gave it a try. The ease of motion made me think of riding a baby calf, and I let my hands go free. "Yee, dogies!" I yelled. "Man, please. Is this all she's got?"

Without warning the machine dipped and bucked, becoming nothing less than a full-fledged bull with dag-gers in his side. When I tried to reach for the rope, the smile I'd been wearing was ripped from my face. Flying upward, I came falling down against the metal saddle, landing smack-dab in the middle of my groin.

I wasn't thrown off, really. It was more like I slid off, rolling around on the blue pad, eye to eye with Ham's silver-tipped cowboy boots. "Ride 'em, cowboy," Ham called out as my father leaned over the riding lawn mower, trying to hide the laughter that caused his shoulders to shake.

Lesson learned, I sort of drug myself over to the side of the mat, legs clamped together. Ham went to reach for the blue blanket and then turned the switch off. "Crank it up again," I yelled while trying to stand upright.

That night as the moths hit against the light that dangled from a ceiling cord, and Shadow barked at the sound of the electric bull, I kept a grip on the challenge. With each jar of my teeth, I came crashing down against the bucking metal saddle, picturing the white spot being torn loose from its hold on my lung. The spot would get knocked higher and higher up my throat and out of my mouth. It would fly into the humid night air to suffocate and disintegrate into the gravel driveway at Rancho FuManChu. One way or the other, I made up my mind I was going to win.

———

The next morning I rose early while my father still slept in the back of the trailer. Thigh muscles that I didn't know I had ached, and it was then that I knew the real reason cowboys were bowlegged. In the back of the camper the beige curtain that partitioned off my father's sleeping quarters swayed to the beat of his snoring.

Outside, the grass was wet with dew, and Shadow only glanced up from his spot underneath the deck of the house. All might have been quiet that morning, but FuManChu was like me, restless. He stopped eating from a bale of hay long enough to snort and look in my direction. When he pranced toward me, the ground shook from the weight of his moves. A trail of fluid ran out of his nose as he stomped against the wooden fence that separated us. We stood there against the purple haze of a new day, eye to eye, watching and waiting. I've come this far, bad boy, I thought. I'm not backing down now. Walking away, I heard him kick the fence once more before trotting away.

Ham had wrapped my hands in tape and gripped the end of a rope, reminding me to keep my thumbs up. My heart beat faster with each swipe of tape that he put around my hand. But it was funny, when I signed the paper saying that he couldn't be sued if FuManChu stomped the living tar right out of me, my heart slowed to a pace meant for an afternoon nap.

My father ambled over with his hands tucked inside his pockets. He looked out into the tall, grassy field that ran out from Ham's house to the edge of the highway. "You sure you want to do this?" His mumble sounded more like a statement than a question.

"Let's do it." Walking to the chute, the word echoed in my head. *"Let's."* There was no *let's* to it. It was me and me alone. But watching the way my father circled the area just beyond the chute and how he kept casting his eyes off toward the field, I realized that I'd used the right word after all. A piece of my father was right up on that bull with me.

FuManChu's muscled back quivered when I eased down on him. The gates of the chute rattled as he tried to twist around in the enclosed area. Pinned against his free will, he snorted and fought to raise his head in defiance to this latest man who was now on his back, trying to break his ego.

"Ready?" Ham asked, holding the stopwatch.

Holding one hand up in the air and gripping the rope with the other, the door of the chute flew open before I could finish nodding. We both came flying out of the chute, kicking. The bull's hind legs flew up in the air, and he jerked his head with a torment that I've yet to see again. Twisting around, I gripped the rope tighter, feeling my neck contort with each strike against his flank. Digging my legs deeper into the side of the bull, I looked down and fought with every bit of spit and vinegar that I had left in me. And all of a sudden, it was not the jerking and twisting head of some bull that I saw: it was the face of Jay Beckett. As I squeezed my legs tighter, the bull snorted and kicked higher until he was almost standing on his front legs. Manure-stained sand was all that I saw when I landed against the dirt, the breath knocked out of me but the spirit stronger than ever.

"Yaaaaa! Yaaa!" Ham yelled from inside the arena, flagging his arms at the bull. At the edge of the fence, my father reached over to lift me, but it was his praise that got me over the fence. "Good job, son. Real good job."

Gasping for air, I tumbled forward and slid over the fence. From the other side, FuManChu raked his horns across the fence and snorted. I looked at the meanest son of a gun I'd ever faced since Jay Beckett and managed to laugh. Laughter continued to ring out as the thing that I thought might kill me trotted away for good.

That night, at a honky-tonk named Road Kill, Ham sucked down Jack Daniels with a frenzy equal to that of his bull. Stumbling up to the tiny stage where a DJ played classic country music, the microphone squealed when Ham snatched it away from the young boy. "I want everybody to listen up," he said, leaning against the DJ's sound system, "that skinny Georgia boy sitting over there . . . Stand up, boy," Ham said, waving his hand and tipping his glass until the drink sloshed to the floor. "That boy just put a natural-born hurting on my prized bull. Fuchow . . . FuManChu." The applause was weak, but my father winked at me just the same. "Come on," Ham shouted. "Let's see how many of ya'll can stay on that bull for 2.7 seconds." And with that somebody yelled, "Play 'Call Somebody Who Cares.'"

A bouncer wearing a black wrestling T-shirt helped lift Ham from the stage, and he meandered through the crowd towards me, pulling something from his pocket. "While you were getting your insides ruptured, I took this picture . . . a souvenir . . . a medal." He tossed a blurred instant photo of me leaning far back, feet in the air, while FuManChu kicked up dirt and twisted sideways.

The next morning, after we'd shaken Ham's hand and paid him what was promised, he reached over and handed me the birdhouse that hung on the deck rail. "Here. A trophy."

Riding down the bumpy sand road, I held the white-steepled birdhouse in my lap and decided that it would go in Grand Vestal's backyard next to her clothesline. She wouldn't know how I came by it. For all she knew, I might have bought it at some roadside stand filled with velvet rugs and plastic flowers. Just as long as my father and I knew the story behind it was all that mattered. That birdhouse would be something that we'd both glance at long after the migrating birds had come and gone. The house would stand as a memorial to the day I broke the phrase "it can't be done."

Taking a pen from the glove box, I wrote on the bottom white margin of the picture Ham had taken, "When life tries to buck you, don't look down and don't give in. Few things are as tough as they first appear."

Addressing an envelope to Malley at Grand Vestal's house, I tucked the photo inside. Life's only worth living if you're willing to share it with the people who matter most.

———

"Are you getting bored yet?"

Heather asked the question twice before I answered. Holding the pay phone closer to the edge of my chin, my two-day-old beard scratched against the receiver. "No, I wouldn't say I was bored." A group of children ran screaming around the chain-link fence that separated them from the booth of pay phones at a campground outside of Amarillo, Texas.

"Well, it sounds like somebody's having a good time," Heather said.

"There're a bunch of kids out here swimming. Man, I wish you and Malley were here. I'm missing you bad."

Looking out into the flat landscape scattered with small oaks and the pink-colored sky that comes with the close of day, I pictured Heather wrapping the phone cord around her wrist and leaning against the wall at Grand Vestal's house, trying to become invisible as she whispered.

"It won't be long," she said. "How's your daddy?"

"Pretty good. He's loosened up a little. Not gripping the steering wheel as tight. Refuses to let me help drive though."

Her laugh was as rich as the sun that was dipping lower across the plain. "Some things won't ever change," she said. "Hey, speaking of change . . . Malley's become a country girl. She's got her fingers all over this farm. She's working that garden like a field hand. I bet we won't be able to drag her back to Atlanta."

"Get out," I said.

"No, I'm serious . . . here," Heather said, handing off the phone to Malley.

While Malley talked of the sale she and Grand Vestal had made at the Farmer's Market and how the row of corn reminded her of green crayons with tips dipped in gold, a light feeling swept over me. I pictured my daughter running through the field of my past, leaves of green slapping against her ankles as she fought her way through the dirt to the other side. Hearing the rise of her voice as she got more excited about doing simple things that I'd taken for granted, I said a prayer right there in front of God, the setting sun, and the squealing children around the pool. With eyes wide open, I thanked the Lord for second chances.

After the call, I walked across the campground. I passed the log cabins and iron picnic tables and felt a change in the wind temperature. Warm, dry air seemed to be tangled inside a cooler current. A piece of crumpled wax paper swirled up into the sky and landed at the edge of the door of the campground laundromat. Inside, a woman with a Dallas Cowboys T-shirt and wet, kinky hair looked at me, her eyes as wild as the wind outside. "It's going to storm," she said, snapping a pair of boxer shorts. "The weather spins on a dime in the Texas Panhandle. It just spins on a dime."

Within two hours that dime must have spun into orbit as the camper trailer shook from the winds and rain outside. Rain fell so hard against the aluminum camper that it sounded like somebody was working it over with an electric nail gun.

While my father pacified himself with the latest western

he'd picked up at the supercenter where we'd bought supplies, I hunkered by the small window by the door. Pulling back the fruit-print curtains, I watched as balls of hail slammed down against the concrete slab around the grill. "Man, it's hailing now."

Not looking up from the pages of the book, my father said, "It'll stop and start like this most of the night."

"For a man whose new trailer is getting whacked up, you don't seem too worried."

"There ain't a thing I can do about it. Besides, around here storms roll in, and just when you think you can't stand it, they roll out." He put the book down on his chest and looked up at the tiny light that glowed above the sofa. "I remember this one time when me and your mama drove out to Fort Carson. We got near here and just did manage to pull into this motor court that an old man and lady ran. Then the rain went to pouring, and the ceiling in our room went to leaking." He laughed and looked at me like I might have been there too. "I was holding up the trash can in one hand and an ashtray in the other. Your mama was running around with the ice bucket over the bed. As soon as one leak stopped, another started. I was fit to be tied . . . mad . . . son, I was mad."

"Sounds to me like you needed your money back."

"Where to go? This was back when motels weren't strung out all over the road like nowadays. Before I knew it, your mama had a kink in her arm from holding the bucket, so we just let the rain pour. We pulled the bed over to one corner, and she told me to close my eyes. Then she put in to telling me a story about Hawaii and waterfalls and such as that. Before she finished I could near about smell the flowers that she claimed she was wearing around her neck. Slept like a baby the rest of the night." He stared into the light and held on to the book that rose and sank against his chest. "The other day ya'll got to talking about missing her. That's what I miss. Nothing fancy. I just miss having her lay next to me at the end of the day."

"She was a good woman," I said, trying not to look at him.

Nodding, my father never looked away from the light, and I got the feeling that if he did, the words would be snatched away. "She was a good wife. Better wife than I was a husband."

A thud rang out louder than the thunder, and we both swayed with the force of the hit. Outside, the sounds of clanging metal and sirens howled in the distance while rain fell sideways. I pushed the door open and saw that the side of the camper was dented. A blue trash barrel was rolling down the driveway. Fighting to close the door, I felt the rain cool the skin beneath my clothes. "The side of the trailer is hit. Looks like a barrel did it."

Sighing, my father looked out from the window. "Always could be worse, I reckon. The ceiling could be leaking."

———

Sunlight spread out across the camper floor the next morning, and the rays slowly crawled up into my bed. Opening my eyes, I ran over to the window. Wet cardboard and Styrofoam containers littered the campground.

Beyond the playground, I saw my father walking toward the camper. He entered and handed me a cup of coffee.

"Looks like she worked it over pretty good last night," I said, running my hand through hair fit for a wirehaired terrier. "I tossed and turned the whole time."

Flicking a packet of sugar against his thumb, he said. "Slept like a baby." He locked the cabinets and got behind the wheel. When we got to the intersection just past the campground, he turned the truck in the direction of town.

"Umm," I said sipping the coffee. "The interstate is back the other way."

"I know it." He flicked a toothpick in the corner of his

mouth. "This road is what they used to call Route 66. What they call the Mother Road. It ain't even on the map no more, but back when your mama and me were driving to Fort Carson, we used to make this track regular. Let's see how much of it I remember."

I made a mental note to mark the date and time of this one down in stone. My father, the man who timed his meals by the second, not by the hunger, was finally breaking free of a schedule. We were taking the long way, through little towns that were no longer fueled by tourist dollars, and down the path that had first introduced my parents to life beyond Choctaw.

That winding two-lane road brought us face-to-face with long-faded billboards advertising everything from pet monkeys to maple syrup. With its curves and postcard-perfect views of valleys dotted with wildflowers, shiny roadside diners, and Main Street storefronts with double-paned windows, the road brought us back to a past I'd never known before. It brought us back to redemption.

Chapter Nine

Past the city limits of a town that was nothing more than a dot on the map, we pulled off onto a gravel parking lot. Red mountains speckled with bright-green pines stood guard over a flat-roofed building below. A tall neon sign flickered with the words Nickel and Dime Diner.

"This place used to be called something else . . . something Mexican," my father said as he pulled the keys from the ignition. "Anyway, we stopped here one time when we were heading back home for Christmas. The Christmas before I took off for 'Nam."

I knew that the subject of war was off-limits. The scar on his arm and the hunk of missing flesh that made my father's back seem unbalanced were the only signs that he'd ever even served in the war. "It's best just to leave some things alone," my mama would say whenever I'd ask about the scars.

A moose head with wide antlers hung on a paneled wall at the diner's entrance. Inside, a woman with a freckled face welcomed us. "We're full at the moment. But feel free to have a place at the snack bar if you like."

We sat on red-vinyl stools at the snack bar and ordered from a menu that was smeared with crayon marks and grease. A young boy with a pencil tucked behind his ear mumbled a greeting and put two glasses of water before us.

If the waiter lacked hospitality, the man sitting next to me made up for it. Wearing a blue baseball cap with gray sideburns sticking out from underneath, the man started talking as soon as he sat down. "Go with the hot roast beef sandwich," he said.

"Pretty good, huh?" I asked, still holding the menu.

The man nodded and smiled, revealing a gold tooth. "Traveling through?"

"Something like that," I said and glanced at my father. He was staring straight ahead with his cap pulled down lower.

"Where's home?"

The question caused me to flinch. Up until now, I would have answered "Atlanta" without batting an eye, but now that place seemed about as far away as the canyon we were in search of. If nothing else, coming back to Choctaw had reminded me that part of me had never really left in the first place. "Choctaw," I said. "A little place down in Georgia."

"I was in the service with a fella from Savannah. Anywhere close to there?"

"No, we're farther south."

"That fella saved my life one time. We were Green Berets." The man fanned his hands in front of him just like he might have a hot plate of food to worry with. "Down in Saigon. Top secret. Sorry, I can't disclose the details."

With stories ranging from evacuations to attempted assassinations, he painted a war story as flashy as any spy novel. Food did not slow him down. He simply spewed food and tales all in one breath. My father never spoke until after the man had picked up his tab and left the building.

"The way I figure it, if anybody's got to brag about war, they ain't got much to brag about," he said, picking up the check.

Questions long held since the first time I saw his scarred back as a child now came to me in waves, teasing me to walk out into the deep end of the past. "Did you want to go? You know, fight the war?"

He didn't answer until he had cranked the engine and we were pulling away. "It was my job. I didn't necessarily want to go and leave my wife and baby boy. But I got called. It was my duty."

Staring straight ahead at the broken yellow line that separated the highway, I was quiet and never asked about the scars. He never told me the details either. With my father, the past was chipped away in pieces, and I was left to arrange them into a story.

"The first time me and your mama made this trip, we were just wet behind the ears. I'd just finished jump school at Fort Benning when we got married." He chuckled and shook his head. "When I got stationed out here in Colorado, I never let on to your mama how scared I was."

A construction crew was working up ahead on the road, and the traffic slowed and then stopped. "You jumped out of planes, huh? I never knew that."

My father turned and looked at me as if I'd said I didn't know that his name was Ron. "You did too."

"No. I . . . you know, wondered . . ."

"Well, I jumped a lot," he mumbled as he leaned forward over the steering wheel and tightened his grip. "I liked it. It was . . . you know . . . fun. I'm talking about the training. Now, when it came time to jumping out of a helicopter in 'Nam . . . it would make the best of 'em pee in their jumpsuits. Especially after seeing your buddy blowed to bits like clay skeet." He glanced at me, and I nodded my head in agreement, thinking that if I didn't show some sort of reaction, he would stop talking.

"Some of the boys took to the bottle over it. But I used

letters to keep me even-keeled. I'd write your mama every day if I could help it. For some reason . . . it was easier for me to say what I wanted to say with the pen instead of my mouth." I felt the sun pour over me through the truck window and tried to imagine my father writing a letter to my mother. "When I got back from 'Nam I kept on writing her letters. Usually on Sundays, while she was at church. I'd slip off to Brouser's Pond and fish a little and write a little."

Racking my mind for any sign of a letter in the chest that Malley had found, I couldn't help but wonder what had happened to this part of my parents—the part that was buried deeper than the bottom of a cedar box full of memories.

That night while I paid for our rental space at a campground just the other side of the New Mexico border, I pulled a sheet of blank paper stamped with the campground logo from the welcome folder. An older lady, wearing a yellow vest stitched with the campground logo, smiled when I pointed to the sheet of paper. "Excuse me, ma'am. Do you have any more paper? Maybe some envelopes too?"

Sitting outside on the concrete picnic table, I smoothed out the paper against the folder. The smell of charbroiled beef rose high above the campers. Looking up, all I saw were portable TV antennas and satellites attached to the tops of expandable motor homes. Open spaces. Where were the open spaces?

Climbing to the top of our camper, I squatted next to the air vent and listened to the sounds of my father moving about as he got ready for bed. The camper door squeaked open and he leaned out, looking for me.

"I'm looking for stars," I yelled down. "Thought they might give me some inspiration to write a letter to my wife."

Nodding, he turned to close the door. "I was wondering. With all that racket you're making up there, I figured I'd look up and find the mother of all squirrels."

After I'd felt the trailer tilt, signaling that he was now in bed, I flattened the paper against the folder the same way I'd done a hundred times before a final exam.

With pen pressed to paper, I sat there under a sky covered with more stars than I knew existed. My father's matter-of-fact words now echoed in my head. *It was easier for me to say what I wanted to say with a pen instead of with my mouth.*

So I just started writing. First about the stars and how I wished Heather was there to see them, and how, if I could, I'd stand up and make her a necklace from the night sky. I wrote until I had three pages filled up with words that should have been spoken long ago.

———

The next morning, the New Mexico sky was tinged blue, a color that reminded me of the bluebonnets that we'd passed along the highway back in Texas. Ordinary things that I'd never even noticed, let alone knew the names of, now caught my attention. Up until the accident and the discovery of the spot, I would have just flown past the interstate with the rest of the drivers, never noticing the beauty that waved against the breeze of passing vehicles.

Now, as we drove along the old Mother Highway at a speed worthy of a Sunday-afternoon stroll, everything in our path was worth investigation. And for the first time I realized that even a mindless act like breathing had become easier since leaving Atlanta.

Pulling into a gas station tucked beneath a cove of rocks, we found an old man sitting on a stack of tires. He wore a gray work shirt with the name Stu stitched across the pocket. Pumping the gas, I waved, and he ambled closer to the trailer, circling it twice before speaking. "You're a far piece from Georgia."

"Yes sir," I said. "We're going to the Grand Canyon with some stops and starts along the way."

He nodded and massaged the crown of his head.

"Is there anything around here we might need to check out?"

Tucking his hands in his pockets, he motioned with his head toward the highway. "When the tourists used to pass through, they'd usually stop at the zoo just north of the red light. But they closed that . . . oh, I don't know how long ago. The woman who owned it had this chicken that would play the piano for a fifty-cent piece. Word is, she financed a move to Scottsdale off of that chicken."

"Really?" I said. "Well, maybe that's what I need. A piano-playing chicken."

The man was still recounting the money I'd given him for the gas when he looked up. "Oh, and there's a hot-air balloon festival every fall. Now, that draws them in. The older people like me like to watch the sky fill up with balloons, and the younger people like you like to jump from the sky."

"Sir?"

"They jump out of airplanes. Two, three, four at a time. Alton Zeller makes barrels of money carrying them up and down in his old army plane. He was a regular Red Baron back in the war."

I moved close to the old man and whispered, "Where did you say we could find this Mr. Alton?"

Alton Zeller's fortune earned taking the bold up in an airplane to skydive must have been spent on the vehicles he drove on the ground. Edges of the vinyl portable car-port flapped against the breeze as every model of Porsche sat underneath. My father walked around the cars with his hands tucked in his pockets as I listened to instructions from a man who wore a gold chain with a diamond-encrusted Z strapped around his neck.

When Z Man, as he liked to be called, asked if I'd ever skydived before, I mumbled but never responded. "If you haven't done it before, you go tandem with my assistant, Jo. You've got experience, then you sign your life away to me and jump alone." He waved his hands in the air, and the diamonds on his horseshoe ring sparkled. "A matter of forms," he said in a thick northeastern accent. Turning toward a group of clipboards hanging on the wall, he once again waved his hands in the air and mumbled something. His hyper movement reminded me of an over-sized flea.

"So, what will it be? Tandem or alone?" he asked, never looking back at me.

"Alone."

Reaching for a clipboard from the wall, he stacked it full of forms and then began flipping through a pile of green jumpsuits. Signing the forms that he handed me, I was determined not to say any more than I had to. I hadn't made it this far to jump out of a plane with a nanny holding my hand. Z Man yanked a suit from the wall of the air hangar just as my father wandered over.

"Try this one. Look, if it doesn't fit, tell me now. Speak up while we're still on the ground. You'll save us all some headaches. No pun intended." He laughed and patted my back. "Okay, sir, we have a nice air-conditioned lounge for you while you wait for your son." He fanned his hand across the hangar to a white door framed in glass.

"Wait?" My father looked at the man as though the Z on his necklace was blinding him. "I've waited forty years to jump again. I'm not waiting anymore."

"Okay," he said in a singsong way. "Sir, are you physically capable? I'm sorry. I have to ask these questions. Insurance, insurance."

My father cocked his cap back and lifted his chin. "Let me put it like this, Z man. If George Bush can jump out of a plane at eighty, I dang sure can handle it at sixty."

The man's necklace swung back and forth as he hurried inside the office to find another batch of release forms.

"You're sure you're up to this?" I asked with a raised eyebrow.

Kicking me in the seat of the jumpsuit, my father grunted and said, "Boy, go on and get your tail in that plane."

The military-style plane made me think of something my father might have ridden back in Vietnam. We strapped on the helmets while Alton's assistant gave us another pep talk.

The roar of the airplane rattled her words until she sounded like she was talking into a fan. Looking over at my father with only the edges of his face exposed from the helmet, I pictured him as a young man, burdened with a wife and child, and fighting to come out alive.

When my time came, I squatted down and touched the parachute case on my back. When I slightly turned, my father grinned the way a father might the first time his son hits a home run. I couldn't believe we were about to jump from a plane, and my stomach turned with anticipation. Right then I knew if the fall didn't kill me, Heather would.

With wind knocking against me, I stood at the opened door and never looked down. Instead, I kept my eyes focused on the blue horizon and wondered if this was how all of creation looked to the eyes of God.

Jumping was not hard after that thought. Jo gave the signal, and I just slipped out. Getting knocked around a couple of times, I tried to focus on the wide-open horizon before me as I fell faster and faster. It was the sound that I would remember. The wind whistled but never roared. I turned my head to look at my father. With his arms outstretched he seemed bigger than life as he gave me two big thumbs up. Letting out a holler that only the wind and God could hear, I felt the blood rush to my face. It was a battle cry of sorts. A battle cry meant for war against the impossible.

When I opened the parachute, I was jerked back for a second. Peace held me like a dance partner, swaying me closer to the ground. The dance floor was a land patched in brown and greens. Landing with a thud against the ground, the sight of FuManChu, the bull, flashed before my eyes. His rump was a heck of a lot harder than the ground. Maybe living on the edge had just gotten easier.

Behind me, my father drifted, pulling his parachute to the left and circling the crew members who waited on the ground. After he landed, he tore off his helmet, and his hair was standing up across his head. "That's how you do it, boys," he shouted to the crew. His deep-bellied howl, a laugh I hadn't heard since before my mama passed away, rolled across the field.

———

All during supper he talked about the free fall and the way he used to maneuver the parachute back in 'Nam. We laughed and joked about my last look at him before jumping. "I started to reach over and see if I needed to change your diaper right then and there," he said. He threw his head back and howled. Rubbing the edge of his beer bottle, he looked at me and smiled. "Naw, but really, today sure was something . . . thank you, son."

Shrugging, I struggled to find the words to respond. I couldn't remember the last he had thanked me for anything.

That night I felt his appreciation wrap all over me. For the first time since he had taught me to fish, we were one and the same. There were no barriers of time and silence. Right then, sitting in that wooden booth at a roadside restaurant with bull heads scattered on the wall, we were becoming the one thing I'd always hoped we could be: we were starting to become friends.

Excitement over the skydive and my father's words kept sleep at a distance. Turning on the small camper light over my bed, I got up and searched for the postcard I'd bought along with a T-shirt that read "I Survived The Z Man." On the postcard that pictured Z Man suited up and standing in front of his airplane, I let Malley know that her daddy and grandpa were now officially lovers of life. We had jumped, and we had done it together. At the bottom of the card I added: "Don't wait for 'one day' to arrive before you jump out into the unknown and live."

Turning off the light, I took my words to heart. Instead of touching the spot against my chest like I'd done every night since first seeing its picture on the X-ray, I closed my eyes and fought to ignore it. A soft breeze brushed against the camper, and the aluminum popped with the movement of the night. I pictured myself riding the wind one more time. Beyond the distance of a whitewashed horizon in my mind, there were no endings. The wind cradled me, and I drifted until peace ushered me into a place of rest.

Chapter Ten

At a state park, we stopped and collected brochures to mark our journey. I pictured Malley using the colored leaflets to make a companion scrapbook to the one that Mama had kept. A scrapbook of things accomplished.

From the pay phone near the restrooms, I watched people stream past the big poster covered with green dots noting walking trails up the side of a desert gorge.

"Are you drinking the tea? You ought to drink it twice a day." Grand Vestal's voice echoed from the phone line. I pressed the receiver harder against my ear, trying to make out her words over the group of tourists who were passing by.

"Yes, ma'am. Every last drop. And to tell you the truth, I don't know if it's the tea or the sense of accomplishment, but I've felt better than I have in ten years."

"I got your cards." Malley said when she got on the phone. "Did you really jump out of that plane on the postcard?"

"If you're asking, yes. If your mama wants to know, I take the Fifth."

But Heather didn't even ask. All she wanted to do was talk about the letters I'd mailed to her. Hearing her repeat some of the words that I'd written made my skin burn with embarrassment.

After the call, I searched the gift shop and found my father holding up a beaded belt with a silver buckle. "You reckon this will fit Malley?"

Nodding, I ran my hand across the surface of the belt. "She'll be tickled. Hey, I need to pick something up for Heather. I'm going to run out to the truck and get my wallet."

"Take your time," my father said, never looking away from the rack of belts.

Through a maze of sweater-clad women older than Grand Vestal, I made my way down the cobblestoned sidewalk. Right when I reached for the door handle of the truck, it hit me. I'd forgotten to get the keys to unlock the thing.

By the time I'd squeezed through the tour group, the keeper of the keys was nowhere to be found in the gift shop. Wandering through one of the paths, I saw his low-hanging jeans and the untucked shirt dangling from his waist. With his back to me, he was leaning against a bank of pay phones.

His words found me before I'd made it all the way. "Yeah, his appetite is strong . . . still seems to give a little when he walks . . . No, no complaints about pain . . . We're singing from the same hymnal, Heather. I want this trip to be for him too."

If the sidewalk had been made of quicksand, I couldn't have felt any lower. His words made more sense than I ever thought they possibly could. Here I was thinking that this trip was about bonding with my father, and all it turned out to be was a last trip for the soon-to-be-invalid. He had made this trip only as my sitter, a job he had most likely been begged to take for the sake of the sickly son that might soon be too far gone.

"I'll call and give you an update from the next town." When he turned to face me, he batted his eyes and stammered. "Uh . . . hey. I didn't see you standing there. I got that belt right here." He held up the gift for my daughter the same as if it had been a peace offering.

"You just felt like calling my wife, huh?"

Shifting his weight, he tried to chuckle. "Oh that . . . just a trip report, so to speak."

"Yeah, well, when did my appetite and pain level become navigators for the journey?"

He turned back to look at the phone and sighed. "You heard all that, huh?"

"I heard enough. Look, I don't need you or anybody

else playing nursemaid for me. So if that's what you're here to do, then . . ."

"Now, don't get all riled up."

"Don't tell me how to act. Look, I'm an idiot, okay? I believed we were taking this trip to . . . I don't know, get to know each other." He just stood there squinting at me like all of the times he'd done in the past. Staring and searching me like he might have just met me for the first time. He never even said a word when I walked away, weaving in and out of the crowd waiting for the park ranger to begin their tour.

Anger brewed hotter than the sun that was baking the rocks and the sand of the desert I was entering. A state park sign pointed straight ahead, so I walked left. The less people I'd encounter, the better off I would be. A rattlesnake slithered off into the distance. Its tracks left curved shapes across the floor, tempting me to follow the trail deeper into the orange-colored sand that lined the landscape.

Looking up at the sun, I opened up my arms and yelled for everything that I was worth. The sound echoed against the rocks, but relief was only temporary. Hot wind brushed up against my face, and the howl it created caused me to turn.

"Sir?" a female park ranger said. "Everything okay?" She moved closer, and I dropped my arms in surrender. No matter how far I might have tried to make it on my own, the part of me that was angry and bitter had taken root too deep inside of me. No place would be far enough to run.

"I just . . . I must've gotten turned around."

Back at the park, I was the one who did not want to talk. I leaned against the passenger door, folded my arms, and counted the road signs to our destination.

"I'm gonna say this only one time. You can't get mad at people for caring about you," my father said.

Driving across the vast space on a two-lane road that seemed like a trip to nowhere, I dissected the notion that Heather and my father had set up the whole trip. I pictured them conspiring the plan as I lay in the hospital: one last trip for the boy before the spot grew up and suffocated his lungs.

At a campground, our trailer rested between a tent and a rock garden. That night, after a meal of silence, I retreated into the night and climbed into the back of the truck, dangling my feet from the tailgate. Bare chested and barefooted, I felt free as I could be in that wide space. Through the front window of the camper, I could make out my father lying on the sofa, reading a Zane Gray novel.

Fishing for a new bottle of tea from inside the last supply box Grand Vestal had packed, my hand landed against soft leather. Pulling out a book, a piece of paper fell free and floated to the bed of the truck.

Through letters that looked like the scribble of a fourth grader, Grand Vestal made her opinions known.

> *Sugar Boy,*
>
> *When we went through your mama's things the other night, I happened to think about her Bible. Your granddaddy and me gave it to her the day she accepted the Lord and got baptized. She kept this book with her all through her life. When the cover wore out, she took it to a man in Valdosta who charged forty-five dollars to fix it! I told her, "Land, child, I didn't pay that much for the book to start with." But she said, "Mama, that book is lined with every tear of happiness and sadness I've had in life. Whatever it was, that book and the good Lord got me through it." Now then, it's time you had this Good Book. I don't mean to preach, but you're searching. I see restlessness all through your eyes. Stop drifting and start leaning. No matter how grown you think you might be, you can't do it by yourself. Nobody can. Let the words of this book be a torch to your path*

*and a light to your feet. That's where you'll find the
land of the living.*

I love you more than you know.
Grand Vestal

Flipping through the pages that were tabbed and lined
with the notes my mother had long ago made, I looked
up at the stars and thought of Grand Vestal's old
preacher, the one with the patch over his eye and the
cockatoo. Remembering the verse he'd recite from the
New Testament about God taking care of the birds, I
flipped to the sixth chapter of the book of Matthew.
There in red letters were the words of Jesus: "Seek first
the kingdom of God and His righteousness, and all these
things will be added unto you." I read the verse six times
and pictured it spray painted across the star lit sky.

Before turning the page, I noticed an arrow pointing to
the bottom margin. Written in blue ink were the swirled
words that my mama had added: *Pray for your inner life:
peace, joy, and love. That's the Kingdom of God.*

———

Somewhere in the night, I reached a point of no return.
Darkness fell over the sky, but light was just beginning to

stir within me. With the rising sun came a rise in my spirit. Words long forgotten from Sunday school lessons and those learned from watching my grandparents and mother washed over me like a current pulling out the trash that littered the shore.

The door eased open, and my father stepped out with a cigarette in the corner of his mouth. His hair stuck out just like the cactus he stepped around.

"Morning," I said.

He scratched his head and kept the cigarette in his mouth as he spoke. "You been out here all night?"

"Yep."

"Doing what?"

"Thinking . . . praying . . . reading." I held up the Bible.

He stepped forward, squinting his eyes. "That's . . . where'd you get that?"

"It was in this extra box of tea."

Snuffing out the cigarette against a rock, my father climbed up on the tailgate. He reached for the Bible and rubbed his callused hand across the surface. "She read this book every morning and right before bed every night. Sickness or health . . . she was married to it."

"The words in there . . . I'd forgotten a lot of them."

"Like which ones?"

"Forgiveness."

He looked at the sandstone mountain across the way. The rising sun created a shadow over part of the mountain while the other half glowed a bright orange.

"I . . . I'm sorry for how I acted yesterday. You know, throwing a fit the way I did," I said.

He didn't look at me. "We all get in spells now and again."

"No, it's more than that," I said. There was a distance in my father's eyes. A place that he had long locked away. Before I could find the key, he turned to look back toward the rising sun. "The thing is," I went on, "I've been mad at you for . . . well, I guess ever since Mama died. And when I found that scrapbook . . . the places she dreamed of going. Well, it just sort of boiled those bad memories up to the surface."

He leaned down and picked up a rock. Rubbing it between two fingers, he looked down at the stone just like it might have been chiseled with the words that he needed to say. "Let me tell you something. I wanted more than anything to take ya'll on that trip. But when the tractor broke down, the bills stacked up. Do you know how little I felt, calling off that trip? I'm man enough to tell you that I felt like a failure. So I made a promise . . . someway, somehow, that gal was going to get her trip. Five years ago we pulled out that old book of pictures and started planning." He tossed the rock to the ground and shook his head. "Then cancer got ahold of her. You don't know how many times I wanted to go back in time. If I had it to do over again, I'd drive right out of that doctor's office the first day he told us and keep on driving. We'd have made that trip come hell or high water."

Nobody said a word as the heat from the sun began to warm us. We just sat there on the tailgate of his truck, watching as the sun spread over the dark places of the desert.

"It's just . . . I never saw that," I said. "Take the night she died . . . it's always bothered me that Mama died alone."

"You don't know as much as you think you do." He choked on the words and turned away. "That night we talked about old times . . . good times. Then all of a sudden she looked at me and said, 'I'm satisfied with my life, Ronnie.' That's just how she put it. She was satisfied with her life."

"But she never even left Choctaw except to go off with you when you were stationed in Colorado."

"Son, she didn't have the life *you* thought would make her happy. But she had the life *she* wanted. She told me. Now, I know what I'm talking about."

A coyote called out in the distance, and the sad howl mirrored my own feelings.

"I should've been there that night." My words trailed off, and I looked at my father for guidance, for reassurance that my absence was not held against me.

"The strange thing is that even after all of those doctors pumped her full of medicine, it's like she knew it was time to pass on, and nothing or nobody was going to hold her back. After we'd talked things over, she reached up and touched my neck." He touched the place again as if the feeling could be captured as easily as her words. "She looked at me and said, 'You go on, now. I need to rest.' 'To rest.' That's just the way she put it. I grabbed hold of her hand and I said, 'I love you, Barbara,' and she smiled. I never said that enough to her. She looked at me and said, 'I know you do, Ronnie. I've always known that.'" He was quiet and cleared his throat. "I walked to the door and looked at her, and she kind of motioned me out and said, 'I'll see you in a bit.' That's just how she said it."

A tear fell from my father's eye, and he looked like a man three times his age. "She left the way she lived, not putting nobody out. Not making a big fuss . . . I don't care if you believe me or not, I wanted to stay. I wanted to."

Reaching over, I squeezed my father's shoulder.

Emotions I'd questioned now ripped through him until his muscles shook. It was all there for me to see in the most naked form, and I was left feeling nothing but shame. Words long scripted for this moment now hung in the back of my throat.

"Your mama was happy in the end because she knew that happiness came from down here," he said, pointing at his chest. "Umm . . . If I just had one ounce of that woman's wisdom."

"You've got more than that."

He looked at me in a way I'd never seen. His eyes seemed to search mine for a glimpse of hope.

"You've got her love, and that never goes away."

Chapter Eleven

Traveling the Arizona back roads dotted with green brush, yellow cactus flowers, and sandstone cliffs, I wondered why I'd never taken a trip with my father before. Why hadn't I suggested the trip in the first place? Why did it have to take a white spot the size of a quarter on an X-ray?

Now his wall of silence that he seemed to need as a retreat from the world didn't threaten me. The traits were as much a part of him as the weathered hands that gripped the steering wheel and the red mole below his ear. Flipping through the gold scrapbook that my mama had buried away, a tinge of sadness came over me and I was once again reminded that this was her journey as much as it was our own.

My mama had learned to accept the unreachable part of my father long before, maybe even on the same drive they took forty years ago to Fort Carson. She was the keeper of the secrets and the mender of wounds. If only she could be here to see us now, at ease in our roles as father and son, roles that we now defined on our own terms.

Grand Vestal always said that events in life happen for a reason. A faded newspaper clipping found in a gold scrapbook had started it all. A journey made only because my mama had been brave enough to share her dreams. Now it was up to me to do her memory justice and to live my life with that same kind of boldness. In that sense I guess my mother had never really left us. She was as much a part of the journey as the camper that trailed behind us, swaying with the breeze of passing vehicles on a hot desert road.

Leaning sideways, trying to glance at the clock on the dashboard, my father swerved just enough to make the right-hand tires leave the road. Dust and gravel flew up over us, and a passing semi blared down on the horn. Gripping the side of the door, I almost reached for the steering wheel. Coughing, he turned and said, "Just seeing if you're awake over there."

"A shake to the arm would work just the same. Hey, what's this fixation you've got going with the clock? It's the second time you've looked at it in less than an hour. If you want to know what time it is, just ask me. There's no deadline to meet."

"Yes sir," he replied in a tone that let me know that he did not appreciate being talked to that way.

By the time our truck had climbed the elevation of the Grand Canyon, my mood had shifted with the cooling temperature. Nervousness wrapped all over me until I felt a tingle snake down my leg. We had spent days on end on this search, and now it was the end of the road, a return to a life measured by time, and freedom challenged by the outside world. Part of me wanted to keep on going and lay claim to the Pacific Ocean.

Views of canyon valleys changed colors from red to brown, all with a shift of the sun. Looking down on the areas that we passed, I was left feeling smaller than I'd ever felt before and hungry for something that food could not satisfy. Running my hand across the gold scrapbook that my mother had kept, I looked out beyond the truck window and pictured myself being molded into the clay-colored landscape.

At the edge of the rim, we parked next to the park lodge, and my father got out, stretching his arms high toward a bushel of white clouds that hung over the parking lot. "Man, man," he said.

My nerves were keyed up just thinking of looking out over the edge of the rim. My own fear of emotion caused me to pull back, and for a second I thought of claiming that I needed to take a restroom break before venturing out among the rest of the tourists gathered at the observation deck.

"I don't know about you, but I need to stop in this place first," my father said pointing to the stone lodge that wrapped around the rim's edge.

Inside, a large pine staircase draped in red carpet swept up to the cathedral ceiling. Pine and rugged stone formed the walls that were mounted with the heads of moose and bear. A group of men with German accents and plaid shorts stood in front of the registration desk, clutching overnight bags. A cool breeze swept across the lobby, and in the back of the building, I noticed a restaurant with windows framing God's handiwork outside.

One of the German men with a bushy gray beard looked up to the top of the open staircase. He laughed and pointed to the balcony. As he did so, everyone else in the group turned and followed his point. Not to be outdone, I moved past the group so that I could get a better look too.

There, standing at the top of the wooden staircase holding a sign with colored letters spelling out "Welcome" were Malley and Heather. They laughed when I stepped backward and stumbled onto a luggage cart. I jumped to my feet and darted off past the registration desk. Jumping up the steps two at a time, I ran an obstacle course over luggage while the women in the lodge looked at me like I was a mountain lion who had found his way into polite society.

"Surprise!" Heather yelled while clapping her hands and laughing. Her body molded into my arms the same way my spirit had molded into the space outside. I held her long and kissed her even longer.

Malley was shaking the sign like a cheerleader in training. She laughed when I hugged her and asked me twice, "Surprised? Did we surprise you?"

"When . . . where did ya'll . . . ?" Words raced through my mind but never met together to make any sense.

Wrapping her arm around my shoulder, Heather pointed past the stair banister and down to the lobby. Standing below the wooden chandelier was my father. He was standing by the registration desk, seemingly lost among the German men who were still looking up at us. "Your daddy called the day after you left Amarillo. He was going on about a motel he and your mama had visited that had a leaking roof . . . And then, out of the blue he said, 'I want you and Malley with us at the canyon.' He said it was his gift. Trust me, there was no talking him out of it. The plane tickets, the car . . . he paid it all."

Nodding, all I could do was choke on the words that I wanted to shout down to my father, who was propped against a column of varnished pine. With his hands in his pockets, he looked every bit like the common man that

I'm sure the people who passed by him thought him to be. He was common to everyone, except me.

With no fanfare, my father shyly smiled, and as he did, I saw a glimpse of the face from the photograph, the face of that skinny army sergeant standing in the middle of the snow with his wife, searching for the hope of better tomorrows.

In the middle of a group of German tourists, my father took off his cap with the faded John Deere logo and tipped it up toward me. He never looked back as he walked outside and turned the corner, moving closer to the edge of the canyon that had been waiting on us for thirty-five years.

———

During a supper of rainbow trout at the lodge restaurant, I tried to toast my father. With the white tablecloths and napkins, he kept his arms folded and seemed uncomfortable, so I didn't press the point. I obeyed the shake of his head and the wave of his hand. Instead, I held up the glass of wine and simply said, "Will you let me say thank you, then? And that . . . I love you, Daddy." His face flushed for the second time that day, and he looked down at the salad plate in front of him. "Here, here," Heather said. "Ditto," Malley added, copying me by holding up her water glass. My father never did respond. He didn't have to. His love was proven by actions, not words.

In our room that night, Heather massaged my back as we sat in front of the picture window overlooking the stars that hung over the darkened canyon. "Your muscles . . . they're so relaxed."

"It's you," I said, reaching up to stroke her hair.

She laughed and leaned down closer until the smell of her perfume made me drunk. "No, it's peace," she whispered. "You're at peace."

"I'm getting there. I'm man enough to admit it: You were right. I needed this trip."

"For your mama, or for you?"

"For me and my daddy. I think Grand Vestal's right. You can know my daddy your whole life and not really know him, but because of this trip, I think I understand him better."

"Like what?"

"That he loved my mother. That he loves me. That he's a good man who's had a tough life. And you know what? That's all I really need to know."

Heather looked out the window. "I'll never forget how he looked the Christmas after your mama passed away. He just sort of stumbled his way through."

Holding her hand, I massaged the tip of the diamond on her wedding ring. "Promise me something . . . if something happens to me." She tried to pull away, but I held her hand tighter. "I'm not saying it will . . . but if it does . . . don't stumble along like that."

She shook her head, and the curls of her black hair danced with the movement. "I can't promise that . . . "

"You can promise that you'll keep on living . . . not just making it . . . but really living."

She ran her finger across my lips until they tingled. "Baby, you can't keep us from hurting. I know what you're trying to do. When I got into this game with you nineteen years ago, I knew what it meant. I knew there would be hurt right along with happiness." I opened my mouth, but she placed her finger back up to my lips. "Nathan, the way I see love is that it's a Ferris wheel. It goes up. It goes down and even circles around, never seeming to end. But sooner or later we're going to have to pay the admission price. To me, love is the same type of ride. In the end it's always going to cost us something. So I'll take my chances."

An outside breeze ruffled the curtains, but I remained warmed by her words. In days gone by, I'd have changed the subject or would have trained my mind to focus on finding a solution to a work project while her words buzzed about me but never landed. Now I was soaking my wife's words into my pores and still hungering for more. Loving me would cost my wife and daughter a price, a price that they would pay out in installments over time. And for the first time, it was a debt that I could not pay for them.

There, inside a lodge on the edge of the Grand Canyon, I fell in love with my wife all over again. Everything about her that I had taken for granted greeted me with a freshness that was as crisp as the air that drifted into our room. And that night I pledged to give whatever number of days I had to her in body, mind, and spirit.

———

When I woke up the next morning, Heather's arm was across my chest. Easing out of bed, I lightly placed her arm across the blanket, and she rolled onto her side. Never waking, her arm spread out across my pillow, and I fought the urge to reach over and run my hands through her hair. But beyond the room there were more bridges to mend, and the job of repairing them had been weighing on my mind for the past few hours.

Early dawn was rolling into the canyon, and the young man at the front desk smiled as I approached. With the exception of a cleaning crew and the sound of a vacuum cleaner, the lobby was empty.

"Do you have any paper? Letterhead or something?" I asked the man.

He never broke his smile as he handed it to me and then continued flipping through the night receipts.

Out on the stone-covered porch I zipped the Windbreaker and wondered how weather could feel so cool in June. A blanket of haze hung over the front of the lodge like a wayward cloud that had lost its way from heaven. I sat in a rocking chair and listened to the sound of birds signaling the start of another day.

For the past week my mama's words from her Bible had stayed in my head, always a reminder of what was meant for kingdom living. *Peace, joy and love—pray for your inner life,* the swirled letters written in the margin of her Bible had said.

Putting pen to paper I wrote, "Dear Jay." I hadn't spoken with Jay Beckett since the day he drove away from my house with the knowledge of the spot that rested in my chest. That day he asked me what I'd planned to do. So now I spelled out the details for him, the journey with my father, the skydiving, the bull riding, and all of a sudden I realized the things I'd done before the accident were nothing more than ingredients for a boring life. But it was the words that I used to close the letter that seemed the most important.

I've been hating you, Jay. I admit it. I was angry for what you did to me, filling my job and demoting me. The bottom line is, it hurt that you didn't have the common courtesy to call or talk with me face-to-face. But I'm putting that all behind me now and I want to thank you. Thank you for giving me the chance to find out what life is really about. If it weren't for the accident, I wouldn't have learned what I know now. And if I'd gone back to work, I'd still be the same man I was, and the fact of the matter is that I don't want to be that man anymore. Forgiveness is only as good as we're able to forgive. So I'm asking you to forgive me for the way I've been feeling about you and for breaking your door that day. I'm sending a check with this letter. Please let me know if I owe any more. You did what you felt that you had to do. Now I'm doing what I feel like I must do.

Louise said I needed to go home and heal, and that's what I've been doing. It's a long story, so I won't go into it now, but things are changing and I like to think for the better. It's not easy letting go of something that's been part of my life for twenty years. But I realize the time has come for me to leave Beckett Construction and start a new life with my family.

I looked over the letter at least a dozen times. Once I mailed it to Jay, there would be no turning back. There would be no job to go to each morning, and most of the employees would probably think that I'd been fired. I tapped the edge of the pen against my teeth and struggled with how to end my letter to the man I'd first met in a dorm room some twenty-two years ago. A cottontail rabbit darted out from the fog and crossed the grass that lined the edge of the porch steps. Before leaving Atlanta, I doubt if I'd have even taken the time to notice such a sight. And it was then that I found the words to close. *Jay, I only hope that one day you'll get the chance to live like you were dying.*

———

The morning that we were to leave, Heather and Malley were standing by the rim of the canyon. Clanging from the pole, a U.S. flag whipped against a breeze meant for springtime.

"Taking one last look?" I moved to allow an Asian couple a photo opportunity. There was a lot to take in. In the last few days we'd crammed as much in as we could, even giving in to Malley's wish to ride to the bottom of the canyon on mules.

My favorite day had been spent fly-fishing along the Colorado River that ran deep inside the canyon. It was the water that first brought me together with my father. As a boy, I'd learned to fish with him at Brouser's Pond. His thick and callused hand showed me how to cast a line, unhook the catch, and clean it for supper. Talk of bait, water levels, and those that got away were all the words we needed back then. Now it would be the water that brought us full circle, students stepping out into unknown waters, casting in ways we'd never tried.

The fishing guide, Hawley, was not much older than I was, but he could make his line sing as it flew across the water; mine always ended up diving and whipping the edge of the bank.

Standing next to my father, grinning at him whenever he made a smooth cast and grimacing when he twisted it in knots, I realized that all of the things that I'd been called after surviving the accident at the plant were now true. I was lucky and blessed all at the same time. I'd been there when this man with the faded green cap had taught me how to do his favorite thing in life, to cast a rod. And

I was there when he was man enough to admit that there was still more that he could learn.

"Words," Heather said, taking that final look at the canyon on our last day. "Words can't describe this place. I feel so insignificant."

Wrapping my arms around her, I could feel the pulse in her neck. Her skin was warm and sweet, and I tried hard to memorize the smell as much as the view before us.

"Look," Malley said. She was standing by a small plaque etched into a stone column of the observation deck.

Heather leaned down lower and read the words aloud. "O Lord, how manifold are thy works. In wisdom hast thou made them all. The earth is full of thy riches."

A silence fell upon the deck, and only the wind could be heard as it lifted our hair and the lapels of our jackets. We stood there one last time, staring out at the greatest sanctuary ever created, and I thanked the Lord for the gift of His beauty in the places and faces that I'd encountered on the trip.

My father pulled the camper trailer around to the side parking lot next to the lodge. It was then that I started to ask Heather to cancel the tickets and to follow us back. But she had her schedule the same as I had mine. There was a high-school reunion in the works, and the Walker twins had talked her into serving on the host committee. She had even mentioned an opening at the high school in Choctaw but never went so far as to say that she was interested in applying. Our future was as wide-open as the canyon we were leaving behind.

"When do you expect to be home?" Heather asked, never realizing that she was now referring to Choctaw, Georgia, as our place of residence.

"A week probably. I don't know; we're men of leisure, remember."

She brushed my face with her hand, and her hair swept up in the wind. Placing my hand against her head, I pulled her closer one last time. "I'll love you long after the cliffs have caved in and the canyon is filled. Don't you forget that."

Heather seemed puzzled as she let go and looked at me, searching me with her dark eyes. She licked her lips and called for Malley. "I want you home, Nathan Bishop. I want you home."

As they drove away to the airport, my father and I watched them go. Malley turned around and faced us as they moved closer to the entrance of the park and then down the highway to our future.

My father gripped the top of my shoulder, gave it a

squeeze, and then cranked the truck. As we drove away from the place that held my mama's dreams and the keys to my peace, I whispered, "Drive slow." The sun flooded the side of the passenger window, and I squinted to make out the red, gray, and orange colors of the canyon. With the shift of the sun, the colors changed just as sharply as the colors in the glass figurines that my mama used to keep on top of the coffee table at our home. Colors that would continue to tint my memories until my last day on earth.

Chapter Twelve

You get to know a person after traveling with him for more than two weeks straight. The time he takes his meals, the way he refuses to drive more than five miles over the speed limit, even the way he holds the steering wheel with one arm propped up against the truck window. Across the miles it's the small things that become tattooed on your mind. The small details fill in the gaps until you're satisfied that you really know the person sitting next to you.

Even though there were some things that we still chose to keep to ourselves, the wall of silence that had troubled me at the start of the journey now seemed a natural part of us. The sound the tires made as we drove over the cracks in the road and the whine of the wind as it sneaked through a leak in the door, those were the sounds that filled the truck. We listened and wondered where we would go from here with nothing left to hide, nothing left to battle. A good kind of tired, the kind that comes from a day of hard, manual work, left me satisfied and hungry for more.

"What day of the week is it, Tuesday?" My father asked while looking at the clock on the truck dashboard.

"Monday," I said. Instead of worrying that he'd slipped into some stage of forgetfulness, I was grateful that time was something that no longer kept a fence around him.

"You think you'd mind if we slipped up to Colorado on the way home?" my father asked. "I've been thinking about that place. I think I'd like to drive past Fort Carson one last time."

Snowcapped mountains stretched over the range, and I wished that Heather and Malley had followed us back home. There was no end to the sanctuaries. They were as plentiful as the denominations that lined the roads back in Choctaw.

Since writing the letter to Jay Beckett, the thought of work had slipped away somewhere in the back of my mind. Now I once again found myself thinking back to work goals I'd made for the coming year. I'd planned to take some of the plant engineers on a rock-climbing trip to the Rocky Mountains. It was to coincide with the sign-ing of our new contract with the mill. I'd even joined a gym and began toning up. Now all those details seemed attached to the life of another person I'd met but never really known. We went higher into the mountains, and as we approached a bend in the road, I pictured myself borrowing my father's John Deere cap and throwing my old goals inside. Rolling down the window, I'd inhale the clean air and then dump the hat's contents down into the valley far below, where buzzards and other scavengers take care of what's no longer alive.

—

We made our way back to Choctaw without realizing that Father's Day was two days away. Grand Vestal's house was dark when the truck lights hit the front porch. As if timed, one bedroom light came on, and then another. Standing on the porch with Heather and Malley, Grand Vestal's white robe and loose gray hair made her look like a ghost with outstretched arms. "Sorry to wake everybody," I said.

Malley wrapped her arms around me while Heather offered a sleepy kiss. We all moved like robots, and for a second I wondered if the entire journey had only been a dream.

After my father left for home, I started to unpack. I found a crumpled envelope, stained and folded in quarters, on the nightstand next to the bed. "What's this?" I asked while unbuttoning my shirt.

Heather walked into the bedroom, rubbing lotion on her hands. She hugged me from behind, and her breath was hot against my ear. "Malley found it when we got back home. It was under the bottom panel of your mama's hope chest. There were all sorts of things. We think she even kept a lock of your hair in it too."

Weariness burned my eyes, but there was no way I would sleep without first finding out what was inside the envelope.

Walking through the house, I ventured to the back porch. Wind rattled the edge of the paper as drops of rain began to land on the porch steps. There was no guessing who had written the tiny words. My heart raced as my eyes soaked up the words like they might evaporate from the page.

Dear Barbara,

What a week we've had. I'm sitting out here thinking what a blessed man I am to be able to welcome my first grandchild to the world. Malley. That's some name, and she's going to be some girl. My heart filled up with the pride of a rich man when you held her and cupped her head the same way you used to hold Nathan. We've shared a lot of good times together, but I got a feeling this little girl will be one of the best yet. We'll watch her grow up into a young woman, and she'll call us Grandma and Grandpa. But I got to tell you, I don't know any grandmas that look as beautiful as you.

When we were driving back from Atlanta, I got to studying about Nathan. I'm proud of our son. He is a self-made man who loves his wife, and he's going to be a good daddy. I'm proud, not because of what I've done, but because of what you've done to help Nathan grow into a man of character. Part of me never knew how to treat him, not wanting him to be babied and turn out soft. The other part of me didn't want to be harsh on him the way my own daddy was on me. I was always worried I'd do him harm in some way and he'd end up feeling the same about me as I did about my own daddy. So not knowing what to do, I made the mistake of doing nothing. I'm man enough to admit it, I love my son. I can only thank the good Lord that you were here to show him your love, and I'm glad that you're here to love me now. You're the center of our family and the keeper of our hearts.

We can't go back in time. You've told me that over and over again. So let's just move forward, sharing our lives with this baby girl. Teach me how to be a good grandpa. Teach me how to show her love.

I love you,

Ronnie

Smoothing out the wrinkled paper, I read the words until they were memorized. Lines from the letter filled the gaps of my story the same way they filled the canyons of my soul. Sitting there listening to the rain fall against the tin roof, I couldn't help but thank God for leading my mama to save that letter, for securing it in a place that the girl it was written about would find it.

Holding the keys to my father's heart, a sense of responsibility fell upon me. The knowledge of just how much my parents loved each other called out a need to protect. Some things should be kept between a man and his wife, my father had told me.

Stepping out into the rain, I held the paper up as water fell across my face and onto my clothes. Washing away the hurts as much as the ink of his words, thoughts meant to be shared only between lovers and life partners smeared until the paper was nothing more than pieces on the ground. The fire of love had first consumed the words my father had written for my mother. Rain now swept the rest of them away.

—

That Sunday after church, we arrived to find my father sitting on the porch step smoking a cigarette. He put it out just as Grand Vestal climbed out the car, pocketbook and braids swinging with her every move. "I was hoping that going on that trip would cause you to give up those cancer sticks," she yelled. "I heard them say on TV that some of those states won't let you smoke anywhere in public."

"Yeah," he said stomping out the cigarette. "That's why I bypassed those places."

Around back, my father had already started the feast. The portable cooker was boiling with hot grease, and the cooler that we packed with dry ice held the modest catch from our attempt at fly-fishing. Lawn chairs were scattered about the backyard as Heather whipped a white tablecloth in the air and smoothed out the wrinkles on the same card table that once held my birthday cakes when I was a boy.

Grand Vestal slowly walked down the back porch, carrying a tray of potato salad and a plate of sliced tomatoes. "It's going to rain again tonight." We didn't bother asking her how she knew. Her answer was always the same. "I can see it in the shape of the clouds."

We're the same as any family on any given Sunday, having a fish fry and celebrating the gift of fathers. I thought of the towns that we passed along the way and wondered just how many of those townspeople were following our example.

After we ate the trout and lingered over Grand Vestal's strawberry pie, we updated them on the trip and the people we'd met along the way.

"Did you really ride a bull is what I want to know," Grand Vestal asked. Holding up my hand, I just smiled and didn't say a word. "I'm of a good mind to get a switch after you," she said. "Now, you know better."

"No, I really don't. And the thing is, if I would have known, I'd have done it anyway."

Malley placed two gift-wrapped boxes on the corner of the table and then looked at us. "Here," she said. "Go on and open them now."

"Malley," Heather said. "We'll do that when everybody's done with lunch."

"We don't have a schedule to follow," Malley said and stepped away to gauge our reaction.

Motioning with his chin, my father instructed me to go first. Tearing into the paper, I found an arrowhead tied to a piece of thick leather.

"It's a necklace. I made it," Malley said.

Grand Vestal moved closer, wiping her hands on a yellow dish towel. "That arrowhead belonged to your great-great granddaddy. And his daddy before him. It was made for survival."

Trying it on, the arrowhead felt cold against my skin. "Well, how about that? This is all right. Thank you. I love it."

"Now your turn, Grandpa."

My father never said a word as he carefully unwrapped the package. His eyes widened in a way that made me think of how he might have reacted to a gift when he was a little boy. Holding up a photo of him and my mother as young newlyweds at the Colorado base, he shook with the memories of yesterday. Trying to speak, he simply nodded his head. Reaching over, I patted his shoulder and then let go as he moved away toward the side of the house.

"Just give him a minute," I whispered to Malley.

"That's the picture that was in the hope chest. The one Malley pulled out that day during lunch," Heather said. "We took it to a studio in Valdosta. They enlarged it and tinted it with color."

Evidently the color was too close to the real thing, because I never saw the photo that afternoon. My father kept it tucked safely inside his truck. Then, once again I recalled his words, "Some things just need to stay between a man and his wife."

———

A lifetime of plans can change in a matter of weeks. After the photos from our trip to the Grand Canyon had been tucked into Malley's photo album, Heather and I made several trips back to Atlanta to visit with doctors and real estate agents interested in listing our house. Whether we would ever admit it or not, Choctaw was drawing us back to a world we thought we'd left far behind.

During our trips back to Atlanta, Malley stayed at Grand Vestal's. At first we thought that her desire to stay was on account of her not wanting to make the trip in the car. But the truth was, my father and Grand Vestal were spoiling her rotten, and she loved every minute of it. My mother would have been proud of my father: even without her guidance he had become a good grandpa.

One Sunday afternoon after we'd gotten back from Atlanta, I leaned back in a chair as my father told our sky-diving story again on Grand Vestal's back porch. I listened while watching Malley move closer to the garden. She ran her hands lightly across a stalk of corn and dug her toes into the edge of the soil. An image crossed my mind of the same scene being played out fifty years ago with my own mother, milling about the garden on a lazy Sunday afternoon. In my mind she is laughing and kicking the dirt high in the air. Suddenly an urge overtook me, and I never stopped to second-guess myself.

Never looking away or answering my wife's question as to why I was pulling off my shoes, I took off running like something gone wild. Feeling the weight of the arrowhead against my chest, I reached my hand out to Malley. Her laughter rolled out in front of me as the tips of her fingers brushed against my palm. Hot dirt from the garden molded against my feet, and the edge of the plants tickled my ankles, teasing me to stay. Breathing echoed inside my ears, and the beat of my heart pounded like a drum calling the untamed.

Open green pastures with a backdrop of thick trees were before me, and the grass was soft against my feet. Running through the earth that was tilled by my past and my future, I looked into the face of the unknown and laughed right out loud. There were no longer any endings, just beginnings.

Running past the clothesline and deeper into the pasture that lined the edge of the barn, I felt myself becoming lighter, until nothing, not even a white spot, could keep me from soaring on the eagle's wing. One with the earth and my people, the arrowhead slapped against my skin. Childhood memories lined the length of my journey, and I pictured my mother laughing and clapping with the rest of my family, cheering me on to victory.

I am home. I am loved, and now I am free.